FORTUNE'S CHILD

Louisa Farnham has settled down con-
tentedly to being an old maid after a
brief, unhappy betrothal in her youth.
Several years have passed since she enjoyed
a Social Season and it is with great
misgivings that she accompanies her sister
to London. Everyone assumed her to be
in town to find a husband. It was enough
to send her scuttling back to the country
on the first coach, only her one-time
fiancé returned to London too and she
was determined not to be seen as running
away from him!

FORTUNE'S CHILD

by
Rachelle Edwards

Dales Large Print Books
Long Preston, North Yorkshire,
England.

British Library Cataloguing in Publication Data.

Edwards, Rachelle
    Fortune's child.

    A catalogue record for this book is
    available from the British Library

    ISBN 1-85389-657-8 pbk

First published in Great Britain by Robert Hale Ltd., 1981

Copyright © 1981 by Rachelle Edwards

Published in Large Print June, 1996 by arrangement with Robert Hale Ltd.

Dales Large Print is an imprint of
Library Magna Books Ltd.
Printed and bound in Great Britain by
T.J. Press (Padstow) Ltd., Cornwall, PL28 8RW.

One

Amy Mulcaster walked swiftly down the upper corridor of her elegant London town house. As she walked, her silk skirts rustled ever so slightly, and whenever one of her housemaids passed the girl bobbed a curtsy, aware that their mistress paused now and then to draw her finger along the tops of furniture in the hope of detecting a speck of dust.

Despite these frequent pauses, however, Mrs. Mulcaster knew just where she was going. Even as she had reached the top of the stairs she could hear the shrill cries of delight which were emanating from the schoolroom at the far end of the corridor. As she pushed open the door she experienced no surprise at the scene before her; five excited children were running hither and thither as a sixth person, blindfolded and looking no more than a child herself, was attempting to catch one of them.

The cries of delight continued as Mrs.

5

Mulcaster, unnoticed by any of them, watched for a minute or two. As the girl in the blindfold finally caught one of the children, to further squeals of delight, Mrs. Mulcaster clapped her hands.

'That is enough for now, children.'

'Oh, Mama,' cried the elder, a girl, 'we are having such great fun with Aunt Louisa.'

Her mother smiled at her fondly. 'So I observe, but Miss Hilton is waiting to take breakfast with you, and I wish to take mine with Aunt Louisa. I trust you have no objections to *my* enjoying her company for a while.'

As she spoke her younger sister pulled off the blindfold, smiling breathlessly as she did so. Her cheeks were flushed and her eyes bright.

'Do as your Mama bids you, children, and if you're good we shall play again later.'

They ran out of the room, squealing and laughing, jostling one another, watched by their mother and aunt.

'You make Miss Hilton's life an easy one,' Amy Mulcaster observed, 'spending so much time with them.'

'Your children are delightful, Amy. All

too soon they will be grown so I must enjoy their company whilst I may.'

She paused in front of a wall mirror to pat her pink cheeks and then to tidy her dark, unpowdered curls. Her eyes still shone brightly with the pleasure the game had afforded her.

'I am so glad you prevailed upon me to purchase new gowns. So many of my old silks are demode now. Everyone wears muslin, 'tis amazing.'

'I told you so.'

'Do you think this new hairstyle truly becomes me, Amy?' she asked after a moment, frowning into the mirror.

Her sister had been regarding her sombrely. 'Indeed it does. Shorter hair is becoming all the crack, and I declare you look no older than Joanna.'

Louisa turned to face her sister. 'I cannot credit that as I am six and twenty, and everyone knows it.'

'Ah, but a stranger would not believe it, I'll warrant.'

Louisa linked her arm into that of her sister and together they began to walk down the corridor.

'It is as well you intervened, Amy, for I declare I am ravenously hungry.'

'I was only surprised to learn you were already risen. We returned home from Lady Procter's prodigiously late and I was so certain you would be abed this morning.'

Louisa smiled. 'It was not my intention to rise so early, but I cannot change my country habits whatever the hour I retire.'

Amy gave her a hard look as they went into the breakfast-room where a cold collation was laid out on the table.

'You look none the worse for it, but that statement reinforces my belief that Mr. Mulcaster and I were perfectly correct in insisting you accompany us for the Season this year.'

'Because I rise too early?' her sister asked in surprise.

'Because you are becoming too rustic.'

When the two ladies were seated at the table, a footman brought fresh coffee, and Louisa commenced to consume a hearty breakfast of cooked meats and bread and butter.

Her sister watched her for a moment before beginning a more modest breakfast.

'Did you enjoy Lady Procter's drum last night, dearest?' she asked in a carefully studied voice.

'Oh, indeed. It was quite splendid. As I recall one may always depend upon her to entertain her guests most royally.'

'She does tend to outshine all others, which I am sure is her intention.' She glanced briefly at her sister before resuming her breakfast. 'I was only sorry Lady Doddington insisted upon monopolising your time with her tiresome chattering. I am persuaded she only served to frighten away any gentlemen wishing to approach you.'

Louisa smiled slightly as she poured out a second cup of coffee. 'It was enough to be present, Amy. After all, I have not participated in a London Season for all of nine years, and I cannot expect all my old dancing partners to rush to engage me, especially as most are now married.' Her sister's lips tightened into a thin line of disapproval but she made no comment for once. 'I can scarcely credit that it is so long since I made my début, and also how much everything has changed. I recall well how I hated to sit for hours whilst my hair was powdered and pomaded into place. Fashion is so much more sensible now.'

'Plain is the word,' Amy told her, not without disapproval. 'Of course, we must blame it on those abominable Frenchies.

Nothing has been the same since the Revolution.'

Louisa nibbled thoughtfully on a piece of bread and butter. 'Lady Doddington declares it could well happen here.'

Amy's eyes went heavenward. 'Lord protect us! We are English! That makes all the difference.'

'*She* declares her servants have become very insolent of late, but I fear she exaggerates. Lady Doddington would find fault with a fat goose.'

'I am relieved to hear you say so,' Amy replied, straightening her lace cap.

For a moment or two they ate in silence, but then it was Louisa's turn to eye her sister critically.

'Amy, you look a trifle hollow-eyed this morning. Perchance you should have stayed in bed a while longer.'

'I shall ride in the Park this afternoon which will soon put back the colour in my cheeks. It is merely an excess of champagne you know. Those fountains at Lady Procter's were altogether too tempting, and Sir Harry insisted upon refilling my glass time and time again.'

'I was obliged to refuse several glasses myself.'

'It is possible your will is greater than mine.' Louisa smiled as her sister went on 'You will, of course, ride with me this afternoon, Louisa.'

'No, dearest, that is not possible. I promised Joanna I would help her with her French lessons this afternoon, and if the girl is so anxious to improve her mind I cannot in all conscience cry off.'

'Louisa!' Amy's cup clattered into its saucer. 'We employ a competent governess for the children. There is no need whatsoever for you to assist.'

'Perhaps not.'

'And as for Joanna wishing to improve her mind...Elizabeth perhaps, but Joanna has nought but windmills in her head.'

'You do her a great wrong, Amy. She is quite set upon speaking French fluently by the end of this Season, and I do enjoy their company so much, Amy. Your children are so delightful.'

Her sister gave her a considering look. 'You've come here to enjoy the diversions and the shops, Louisa.'

'And so I shall, my dear. Indeed, I *do*, for I had almost forgotten what it was like, I confess.'

'That,' Amy answered emphatically,

11

'may not be a bad thing, after the way that dreadful man...'

She broke off abruptly, biting her lip, but Louisa gazed at her across the table, her eyes wide.

'Are you referring to Lord Rossington, Amy?'

Once again Mrs. Mulcaster bit her lip. She was forced to avert her eyes from her sister's. 'I do beg your pardon, dearest. I did not intend...'

'You have no need to beg my pardon, nor is there any need to avoid speaking his name, just because we were once briefly betrothed.'

'Oh, Louisa, I am out of patience with you! The man was—is for all I know—a monster to have used you so.'

Louisa laughed. 'Amy, my dear! He was a perfectly nice young man.'

'Who, once he discovered Papa had lost his fortune, promptly deserted you. A poltroon.'

Louisa gave her a steely look. 'Amy, let us be clear upon this matter. It was I who decided our betrothal must end.'

Her sister's lips remained tight. 'That is the story which was given to the world, and he was man enough not to gainsay it, but we know differently, do we not?' It was Louisa's turn to avert her eyes. 'Oh, my dear, I am so sorry for awakening such horrid memories. I have forsworn to make any mention of it these past nine years.'

'Amy,' Louisa answered in a slightly strangled voice, 'it is of no consequence I assure you. Lord Rossington means nothing to me and the mention of his name cannot hurt me.'

Her sister smiled with relief. 'In that event I can only be glad I did. I had no notion how you felt about him after all this time.'

Louisa gave her a sweet smile. 'Now you may rest assured that I do not pine. I scarce give him a thought, nor have I since we parted.'

Mrs. Mulcaster looked even more relieved. 'How splendid you are, my dear. So many women would have resented bitterly his treatment of you. Ah well, at least we may be sure there is no chance of meeting him whilst you are in London, otherwise nothing would have induced me to persuade you to come.'

'I recall his country estates needed much attention, but in nine years he has had time to put them to rights.'

13

Relief at her sister's attitude to her one time fiancé made Mrs. Mulcaster garrulous. She laughed. 'Do you not know what became of him?'

Louisa shook her head. 'I never much cared. Is that not a dreadful admission?'

'Fudge. It is quite understandable. We shall not talk of it again.'

Louisa chuckled. 'Now you have awoken my curiosity I beg of you tell me why he is not to be found in London this Season.'

'Not on this or on any other occasion. Soon after your betrothal was ended Rossington accepted a diplomatic post in St. Petersburg. According to the tattle-boxes he has been exceeding successful—a favourite of Queen Catherine would you believe?'

Louisa smiled slightly as she pushed away her plate. 'Oh yes, I'd believe it. He had a deal of charm when he chose to exert it.'

'According to Mary Calverswell he exerted it well enough and rumour has it he and Queen Catherine...'

Amy's voice faded away with embarrassment and she began to toy with a piece of bread and butter. Louisa looked at her with interest. 'So they became lovers?'

'Such talk is unbecoming an unmarried woman. I should not have mentioned it. Mr. Mulcaster would give me a severe set-down if he came to know of it.'

'Tush, Amy. I know perfectly well such things happen, but the Russian queen is rather old.'

'Nevertheless...'

'Did he not...marry?' Louisa asked after a moment's pause.

'Yes, so I have heard. To a Russian princess,' she added, almost in a whisper, 'and no doubt she was of wealthy origins.'

'I'm persuaded Lord Rossington could not have afforded to do otherwise.'

'You have no notion how delighted I am to learn at last that you have recovered from his brutal treatment of you,' Amy went on in a high, bright voice.

Louisa answered with a protesting laugh. 'You malign him, my dear, I assure you. The ending of our betrothal was quite a civilised affair. If you had not been at Levenham awaiting Julian's birth you would have realised it.'

'You are too kind for your own good. At least I can be assured that you will

15

not allow the experience to prevent you accepting the attentions of another gentleman should the opportunity present itself whilst you are here.'

'Is that why you prevailed upon me to come with you to London this Season?'

'It is certainly one of the reasons. At your age, it is time you were wed.'

'Do you and Oliver wish to be rid of me?'

Amy's laugh echoed around the room. 'La! What a notion! My dear Louisa, you are a joy to us and a delight to our children, but it is only natural for you to have a home and family of your own.'

Louisa put her hand out and covered her sister's with it. 'Dear Amy, do you not realise that at six and twenty I am an old maid?'

Her sister looked horrified. 'Louisa! What a thing to say! Indeed you are not. Many a worthy female remains unmarried until they're your age. You are a handsome woman, and many a gentleman will gladly pay court to you.'

'For a woman without a portion, only old roués or gouty widowers, and I am not desperate enough to accept one of them.'

'Tush! There are many men of address who would admire a woman like you. And as for a portion, Mr. Mulcaster would not dream of allowing you to go to your husband penniless.'

'You are both too kind to me already; I would not dream of allowing such generosity. After all, you have three daughters of your own to settle...'

Their conversation was interrupted, most welcomingly as far as Louisa was concerned, by the arrival of her rather hollow-eyed brother-in-law.

He greeted them both, kissing first his wife and then his sister-in-law. As they began to reminisce about the previous day's events Louisa made her apologies and left the room, unaware that her sister was watching her worriedly.

Later that day, after Mrs. Mulcaster had left for her ride in the Park at the fashionable hour—not before entreating her sister once again to join her—Louisa made her way towards the nursery suite. Her conversation with Amy had not disconcerted her greatly, for as she had declared it had been nine years since her dazzling début into Society, and she would not wish to be a part of that scene again.

Participating in some of the social events of the Season she had observed such débutantes standing together in groups, wearing their finery, chosen to outshine all competition, and at the same time affecting not to notice the young men of their choice.

Louisa recalled all too well the excitement of anticipating which personable young man would address himself to which hopeful girl. Such joy when the object of one's desires lived up to expectation, such despondency when he did not. It was a relief, Louisa thought, to be freed from that tyranny.

She paused outside the schoolroom, smiling to herself. Married or not, the past nine years had been happy ones and she would not wish to enjoy such foolishness again, although she could not help but recall the pleasure of standing up for every dance and having a queue of eligible young men eager for the honour of taking her into supper.

As she was about to go into the schoolroom she paused yet again on hearing Joanna's voice.

'I don't know where I prefer to be—in London or Essex,' she said plaintively.

'I prefer London by far!'

Louisa immediately recognised the voice as belonging to twelve-year-old Elizabeth. It always amazed her how different these two sisters could be; the one gentle, the other abrasive. Their hopes and aspirations quite different too.

'There is so much to do here in London,' Elizabeth went on. 'It cannot compare with Levenham.'

'There is not a great deal for us to do here,' Joanna replied. 'We must attend our lessons and go everywhere with Miss Hilton. We are not free to enjoy all the diversions like Mama.'

'You, at least, cannot mind it. You have asked Aunt Louisa for extra French lessons.'

Joanna giggled. 'There is a reason for that.'

'You wish to become a blue stocking and frighten away all the young men.'

'No, silly, you are quite incorrect. You see, in two years' time I shall be making my début in Society...'

The thought gave Louisa a nasty jolt.

Soon Joanna would be no longer a child, and the others will also grow up quickly.

'I cannot see the connection.'

Joanna giggled again. ''Tis obvious, you goose. Since the Revolution in France, London has been swamped with émigrés from the Terror. Handsome young *ducs* and *marquis*. How much more interesting they will find me if I can converse with them in their own language!'

'But they all have pockets to let, Joanna. You wouldn't wish to marry a basket scrambler.'

'Not all of them are penniless, but that is of no account to me. Love is all important, Elizabeth. *L'amour.*'

Louisa smiled to herself again. Joanna was indeed growing up. She wondered if, perhaps, one particular *duc* or *marquis* had taken her eye already.

'Naturally, there is a place in one's life for such emotions, but I shall marry for position,' Elizabeth declared. 'A duke, of course, and you will call me Your Grace.'

'We shall see. A duke will first have to make an offer for it to be accepted.'

'I have no reason to doubt an offer will be made. I already know several heirs to dukedoms—English ones, naturally. I should dislike intensely to be leg-shackled to a penniless émigré.'

'*You* may not marry at all. You can be quite disagreeable when you choose.'

'And if *you* persist in looking so moonstruck you may end up like Aunt Louisa.'

Louisa stiffened at the unexpected mention of her own name in this childish conversation.

'Hush, you wicked creature. You must not talk of Aunt Louisa in such a manner.'

'I speak only the truth and have no wish to malign her, you may be sure.'

'You know nothing about the matter.'

'I heard Mama and Papa talking about it once. She was jilted, you know.'

'Of course I know, you goose, but it was she who gave him up. It was very romantic. I can only admire her. I should not have had the courage.'

'Tush,' Elizabeth said scornfully. 'When Grandpapa lost his fortune at gambling, Lord Rossington no longer wished to marry her. She was very brave about it, and *I* can only admire her for that.'

'I wonder if he broke her heart.'

21

'No, silly. If he had she would have *died*. In one of the novels I read the heroine faded away for love of the hero who had abandoned her.'

'Brave or not, I should hate it to happen to me. She had lots of other suitors, you know, so 'twas truly an unfortunate choice, although I cannot blame her for accepting that particular offer.'

'How so?' Elizabeth asked, looking suspicious.

'I recall well some of those who paid court to her and Lord Rossington was by far the most handsome. I recall seeing him on one occasion and he smiled at me and let me listen to his time-piece which made a tinkling sound on the hour, but I didn't see him again after that one occasion. Poor Aunt Louisa. Do you think she still wears the willow, Elizabeth?'

Louisa didn't wait to hear the girl's reply, for she moved away quickly, stung by her niece's attitude towards her. Poor Aunt Louisa, echoed in her ears. Poor Aunt Louisa indeed! So that was how the children looked upon her. It was a revelation to her, and a disturbing one at that.

Two

The rout held at the home of the Earl and Countess of Tainbury was acknowledged to be a huge success even before it was half over.

Hundreds of people milled around the main salons availing themselves of the plentiful champagne which flowed unabated despite the war with the French. Those who wished to do so danced to a full orchestra whilst others played whist or hazard in the side-rooms.

Louisa had been engaged for several dances, much to her delight, although her partners were mostly the elderly roués or widowers she disdained so much. However, the occasional old beau was glad to renew her acquaintance.

It was interesting to see so many of her old acquaintances and the marriages they had made. So many plain heiresses had been elevated to high positions, whilst the prettier but less well-endowed invariably made mundane matches.

Most of her contemporaries were the mothers of a considerable brood of children, and consequently their once sylph-like figures had thickened giving them a matronly appearance. Naturally Louisa, who had no children and did not drink or gamble into the early hours of the morning, retained her youthful figure. Her eyes were always bright and, in the absence of paint, her skin remained flawless.

Lacking real vanity, Louisa nevertheless was pleased with the way the passage of years had treated her, although she still smarted at the conversation she had overheard. She told herself it was merely children's thoughtlessness, but all the same she wondered how many other people pitied her; Amy and Oliver too, no doubt. What was most annoying was the fact that she had never felt sorry for herself. She had always regarded herself as the most fortunate of women despite her unmarried state.

As she was returned to her seat after standing up to a country dance with a Mr. Stephens, whose pink coat with its huge paste buttons offended her sense of fashion, she saw approaching an old acquaintance, once Daisy Dunscombe she was now

Lady Fermoine and very conscious of her elevated place in Society.

'My dear Louisa, how splendid you look tonight. I adore china silk. Obviously it is from Copelands in Bond Street who also happen to be my own personal mercers.'

'It was purchased from Langtons in the Strand,' Louisa replied, knowing that this was precisely the information for which the woman was fishing.

Lady Fermoine fanned herself furiously and gave a rather high-pitched laugh which caused the feathers adorning her hair to tremble violently.

'Ah yes, now I realise it. Their merchandise has improved of late, I own. It is good to see your sense of style no less abated. You were always in high feather, my dear.' She laughed again, disparagingly this time. 'There were several occasions when I actually envied your taste. Nine years is, of course, such a long time to be absent from the *ton,* and everyone has such a short memory, I fear.'

'To me it seems like no time at all, and I have been well occupied, never you fear.'

The woman smiled sweetly as she swished her fan to and fro and looked around to ascertain she was the object of interest.

'Indeed, that is so for me too, but then I have spent so much time in child-bed.'

'You have a family,' Louisa said, warming to the subject.

'Four still alive. Two of them boys.'

'You must be very proud.'

'They are fine children. A nursery must always be full in my opinion. It is a wife's duty after all. La! Time has not been idle for me,' she said with some satisfaction, and then, 'If anyone had wagered that *you* would have remained a spinster no one would have taken him on.'

'Fate is often capricious,' Louisa answered, her tone muted now.

'Oh, indeed it is. You were set to make the most brilliant match, although my dear Mama always did say you had a mite more independent spirit than was seemly in a young lady.

'Did you know Harriet Forbes ran off with her father's valet?'

At this news Louisa was forced to laugh. 'You do not surprise me, for I recall she was always a goose-cap. I have lost track of so much since I went to live at Levenham.'

'I shall have to call upon you at Park Street one day and help you catch up on all the on dits.'

Louisa was saved the trouble of replying, for Lady Doddington stomped up to them. At any other time Louisa would have groaned at this old bore, but on this occasion she was rather relieved at the interruption.

'Poor old Crumpton's just lost his yacht to Grimsdyke who hasn't a penny piece to spend on its upkeep. Gambling's the very devil.'

Daisy Fermoine gave her a malicious look. 'I recall you were always fond of a wager, Lady Doddington.'

'Not any more, m'dear. Not since my wits were blunted by age.'

She laughed harshly, and then Lady Fermoine was claimed for the minuet by an admirer. Both Louisa and the ageing marchioness watched them take their place in the set.

'I remember when you both made your débuts. You were the handsomer by far and still are, I may say.'

'You are very kind, ma'am.'

'I'm not an idle flatterer, as I am sure you know. Well, everyone of us settles

27

down in time, I'm persuaded. Even young George is going to marry, and not that Papist Mrs. Fitzherbert either. Caroline of Brunswick is coming to England to be his bride, and she is a real princess.'

'I am sure His Majesty is very pleased, ma'am.'

'Oh, he is, but the Queen I regret to say, is not. No, by jove. And now we have trouble with the Frenchies again.' She shook her head. 'Such a troublesome race. We have this Bonaparte creature to contend with. A Corsican upstart in the place of King Louis. It's a bad business. I don't know where it is like to end.' She peered myopically at Louisa then through her quizzling-glass. 'Come to Town husband-hunting, have you?'

Outraged at such a suggestion Louisa cried, 'No, Lady Doddington, I have not!'

The old lady laughed again. 'Mrs. Mulcaster's on the hunt, if you're not, so be warned; she means to set you up in your own establishment whether you'll admit it or not. You're not a blue-stocking, are you?'

'No,' Louisa admitted, lowering her eyes.

How she wished she had, after all,

resisted the temptation of coming up to Town. The enjoyment of the shops and diversions had been severely blunted by everyone's attitude towards her. At her age she had no notion anyone would consider her marriageable.

'Take my word on it, my dear, you will end this Season leg-shackled.'

'Oh, I would not depend upon it, Lady Doddington,' Louisa replied, flicking open her fan to disguise her pink cheeks.

'You'll do some man proud,' the dowager went on relentlessly. 'As long as you're not too choosy and you don't let the past deter you. Bad business that, I don't deny. Had Rossington marked as a laudable fellow. Acquainted with his parents, of course, so I never thought he would be such a scapegrace...'

'Lady Doddington,' Louisa broke in quickly, 'I notice that Mr. Macready is beckoning to me. He has engaged me for the minuet and I quite forgot about it.'

'Run along, my dear,' the marchioness urged, and gratefully, after bobbing a curtsy, Louisa did so.

She had no engagement with Mr. Macready who was probably involved in a game of whist in one of the side-rooms, but she could bear the marchioness's tattle no longer. Her cheeks were pink, and as soon as she reached the next room she sank down into a chair and began to fan herself with more fury than was really necessary. After nine years she believed she had a right to expect every one had forgotten her brief connection with the Earl of Rossington.

As she continued to fan herself furiously she received her share of curious looks, but affected not to notice, and after a while Amy discovered her sitting in a corner.

'Louisa, my dear, what are you doing hidden in a corner like this?'

'Hiding from garrulous dowagers,' was the tart reply.

Mrs. Mulcaster smiled. 'Lady Doddington can be trying, but she is influential. It would not do to offend her and always wise to cultivate her friendship.'

'I am not in need of influential friends.'

'None of us can afford to scorn them.'

Louisa smiled. 'Rest assured, Amy, I have not offended her. She believes me to be with Mr. Macready and is ready to give me a wedding-veil.'

'I can quite see how that has put you out of countenance. Mr. Macready indeed.'

'You should not be surprised. After all,

you must be as aware as I that everyone believes me come to London to find a husband at last. Oh, it is beyond all reason.'

Her sister was momentarily taken aback before answering. 'It is not such an impossible feat to achieve whilst enjoying all that the Season has to offer in the way of diversions.'

Louisa gave her a wry look. 'Dear Amy, you are quite transparent to me, you know. You are as skilful a matchmaker as anyone else.'

'Well, is it not natural that I wish you to enjoy the benefits of hearth and home?'

Louisa sighed. 'You mean well, I don't doubt, but, Amy, I have no heart for it. The débutantes are so young, they make me feel ridiculous, and as for those matrons in pursuit of their second husbands... Really, my dear, I think I would be far happier back in Levenham.'

Amy's eyes opened wide in horror. 'Oh no, don't say such a thing. You cannot leave now, Louisa; the Season is but begun and there are so many diversions to come. We have invitations enough to engage us for months. This is all my own fault. It was my mention of that dreadful man the other morning which has overset your sensibilities...'

'Don't be a goosecap, Amy. You did no such thing, and I would be most obliged if you would refrain from calling Lord Rossington "that dreadful man".'

'I am unrepentant. I can plainly see that he has soured your attitude to all men... Oh, here comes Sir Peter Fairchild. He mentioned earlier wishing to take you in to supper...I do hope you will not refuse him.'

'Sir Peter is an old and valued friend of the family and I would not dream of offending him.'

Sir Peter bowed low before the two ladies. 'By your leave, Mrs. Mulcaster, may I have the honour, Miss Farnham?'

'Indeed you may, Sir Peter,' Louisa replied, getting up from her seat and casting her sister a knowing look.

Mrs. Mulcaster looked strained, but drew a sigh of relief when her sister went with him quite amicably. In fact Louisa always enjoyed Sir Peter's company. He was a bachelor of long standing, being well into middle age. As a friend of Oliver Mulcaster, Louisa was well acquainted with him and was normally at ease in his company, but on this occasion felt many speculative eyes upon them.

'Tell me how are you enjoying the Season?' he enquired when he had procured for her a substantial supper.

'It is quite different to my first Season which,' she added with a laugh, 'was also my last. I must admit I don't find it quite as diverting as I did then, for reasons which are obvious to all.'

He seemed disconcerted by her frankness, often held to be a fault, but it was one she could not mend.

'Your frankness, Miss Farnham, is a rare quality,' he answered after a moment.

Louisa was unabashed. 'You are very kind, Sir Peter, but many would not hold it to be a quality.'

'Equally there are many who do; myself amongst them.'

'I am not out of the commonplace, I assure you.'

'In many ways you are. There are those with greater beauty, without doubt, but you have much finer qualities.' She looked up at him questioningly and he went on quickly, 'Oh, I speak as an old friend, my dear, so I trust you will not take offence.'

She smiled. 'Not with you, Sir Peter.'

'During your first—and last—Season, how many offers of marriage did you receive?'

Startled, she answered, 'I cannot exactly recall.'

'Several, I am certain.'

'Oh, indeed.'

'And yet the one you chose ended most unfortunately.'

Louisa swallowed her food and looked at him again. 'My father wished me to marry the man of the highest rank. They were also well acquainted, and being visitors to certain gambling establishments they were in each other's company often. Papa was very anxious for me to marry Lord Rossington, so it seemed the correct thing to do at the time.'

'Well, at least now you are free to make your own choice.'

'The choice no longer exists, Sir Peter.'

He looked shocked at her pronouncement, which amused her. 'I would not say so, Miss Farnham.'

'I discovered something the other day.' He gave her an interested glance. 'My nieces pity me.' She laughed lightly. 'I confess the discovery shook me out of my complacency, Sir Peter.'

'What do children know or understand? Just look around you, Miss Farnham. How many people here are happily wed? Most marriages were arranged like your own, but for them there was no opportunity to escape the prospect. So they live lives of relentless pleasure, in order that they may forget their unhappiness for a little while.'

'Oh, do you really think it is so?' she asked in surprise.

'For many people it is, Miss Farnham. The wives are envious because their husbands support a cyprian, and the husbands resent that their wives lavish affection upon a cicisbeo. Are we not more fortunate than they, Miss Farnham?'

'Oh, you are far too cynical. You surely exaggerate.'

He grinned engagingly. 'Not a great deal, I fear.'

Everyone was beginning to move back into the other rooms, and Louisa relinquished her plate, feeling a trifle melancholy.

'I have shattered your illusions,' he said gently.

'No, you did not,' she replied, casting him a smile. 'I do realise some alliances are miserable affairs, and I was determined to avoid such a fate myself.'

'Very wise. Come,' he said then, 'I shall escort you back to the ballroom and then join Mulcaster playing whist.'

Relieved at the change of subject Louisa ventured, 'I do hope my brother-in-law is not playing too deep.'

'Not compared to some.'

'I have heard that a yacht has changed hands already tonight.'

'Followed by the wretched fellow's country estate.'

Louisa looked away. 'How foolish it is.'

They were walking back through one of the side-rooms when Louisa saw Lady Fermoine coming towards them. The countess smiled and waved to Louisa who was just in the process of waving back when her hand and her smile froze, for Lady Fermoine was clinging onto the arm of a man she recognised immediately. The shock of it made her stop. She blinked too, for she could scarce believe her eyes. The man onto whom Lady Fermoine clung was none other than the Earl of Rossington.

Louisa was rooted to the spot aware only of Daisy Fermoine's knowing grin and the fact that several score people were witness to Louisa meeting for the first time in nine years the man to whom she was once betrothed.

There was no escape. Louisa knew with sickening dread that she must face him, and in front of several dozen people, which was the worst aspect of all.

Relentlessly Daisy Fermoine came forward, and she at least appeared to be in high spirits.

'My dear Miss Farnham, just see who I have here. A very old friend of yours, I am persuaded.'

Louisa immediately sank into a deep curtsy and was glad of the opportunity of averting her face which she was convinced must have betrayed her astonishment. When at last she forced herself to look at him she noted with some surprise that he had scarcely changed, although he seemed to be taller and definitely broader. His hair was thick and curly, but short now, no longer tied back with a ribbon or hidden beneath a powdered wig on formal occasions. His sense of style had improved considerably, for his dark evening-coat fastened by small gold buttons was the height of fashion and elegance as was the shirt which sported only a modicum of lace at the throat and wrists.

When Louisa had known him before his resources did not stretch to the finest clothes or the best tailor. No doubt his marriage to a Russian princess had altered that circumstance.

When she did finally look him directly in the face it was wearing the inscrutable expression with which she had become familiar. His dark eyes betrayed nothing, although he did appear to be looking at her with more haughtiness than he ever displayed before.

As Daisy Fermoine made the introduction, he bowed stiffly. 'Your servant, ma'am.'

Sir Peter looked embarrassed, the countess triumphant. Louisa did not doubt that this meeting was deliberately engineered by the woman, and the resulting *on-dit* would elevate her to the forefront of any conversation in the days to come.

Just as Louisa was frantically wondering what to say, he bowed stiffly once again and he and the countess moved on, but not before Daisy Fermoine cast her a look of malicious amusement. The encounter had lasted no more than a minute or two, during which everyone in the room seemed to have become silent. Then the chattering started up again in earnest, and Louisa was in no doubt about what they were talking.

'My dear Miss Farnham,' Sir Peter began in a shocked whisper. 'I had no...'

Louisa turned to him immediately. 'I beg of you do not trouble your head, Sir Peter. There is nothing to get into a pucker about.'

'Do you wish to leave? Shall I...?'

She laughed then. 'Indeed not, Sir Peter. The evening is not over.'

He was looking at her anxiously, something which warmed her. 'I cannot believe that this meeting has not caused you some small discomposure which you bear well, so you will forgive me if I smile and laugh in order that those who are presently quizzing us shall have nothing undue to note.'

Louisa smiled gratefully and touched his hand. 'Sir Peter, you are a dear.'

Then she saw Amy pushing her way through the crowd. Observing her wryly Sir Peter said, 'I believe I had best leave you two ladies to your discussions.'

Without saying a word, but first glancing around the room in exasperation, Mrs. Mulcaster drew her sister into the hall where they could enjoy more privacy.

'I cannot conceive this dreadful thing that has occurred. It is like a nightmare. I am informed that creature, Daisy Fermoine, deliberately put Rossington in your way.'

'We did meet,' Louisa answered with more calmness than she truly felt, for the encounter had shaken her, coming so unexpectedly.

'Oh, my poor, poor dear, what did that scoundrel say to you?'

'If it is Lord Rossington to whom you refer, Amy, he said very little and I confess I said less.'

'Louisa, you must believe I had no notion he was in England, let alone in London.'

'I do believe it, Amy, and I also believe you are making too much of this. Pray be calm. I have encountered several gentlemen who were once my suitors since coming to London, and that did not cause you to have an attack of the vapours.'

'This one is different. Everyone must know how shabbily he treated you.'

Louisa flicked open her fan. 'I fail to see what that signifies nine years later.'

'You are an angel, Louisa, an absolute martyr!'

Louisa stifled her own irritation as her sister cried, 'Oh, here comes Mr. Mulcaster. Oliver, you look exceedingly miserable.'

'Lost my purse at whist, don't you know?'

His wife sucked in her breath and then, glancing at her sister, said, 'Then perchance you will not object if we leave now; Louisa is feeling quite done-up.'

He looked surprised. 'Are you, old girl? Not used to late nights. Never mind, I'll get the lackey to summon the carriage.' He was about to amble off, rather unsteadily, when he turned back. 'I say, Louisa, you'll never guess who I saw just now.'

Amy glared at him, and, drawing a sigh, Louisa answered, 'Oh yes, I can!'

Three

'I suppose you'll be more determined than ever to return to Levenham now.'

Amy Mulcaster looked at her sister as they travelled in the family landau towards Oxford Street the following morning. It was

41

the first time she had even broached the subject of the previous evening's events, preferring to wait until they were alone in the carriage with no chance of interruption, and her sister had exhibited no inclination to discuss it.

Louisa, much to her sister's relief and surprise, looked as she always did, calm and sensible. There were no tell-tale shadows beneath her eyes which sparkled brightly when she turned to look at her sister.

'Oh, I cannot go to Levenham now, Amy.'

Her sister looked bemused. 'Why not?'

'Everyone will say that I am running away from Lord Rossington, which would not be true.'

'Tush to the tattle-boxes.'

'Precisely my feelings. Let them do their worst. It is of no account to me, but I will not stand accused of turning tail.'

'But, dearest, you are bound to come across him at every turn. Every hostess who has issued an invitation to us is certain to invite him too.'

'They will have poor sport. We shall treat each other as civilised strangers, which is precisely what we are. It will be most disappointing, I vow.'

Mrs. Mulcaster sank back into the squabs. 'I am exceedingly relieved to see you in this mind, Louisa, although in truth you puzzle me.'

Louisa smiled. 'Surely *you* did not expect me to have an attack of the vapours.'

'Well, no but...'

'Or be prostrate with grief in my bed this morning? Oh, Amy, you are a romantic at heart. I cannot believe I am expected to wear the willow for him.'

Mrs. Mulcaster shifted uncomfortably in her seat. 'I am sure I do not expect anything of the sort, but there are many who do.'

'I vow I shall give them no cause to derive amusement from this situation, although in truth I find it vastly diverting myself.'

'You have grown exceedingly hard.'

'You know I never gave him my heart, Amy.'

'So you have always declared, but as I said to Mr. Mulcaster at the time, I could not conceive of you marrying any man merely to please Papa.

'I must confess,' she went on after a moment's pause, 'he looked very well last

43

night. Quite the bang-up blade, don't you think?'

'Lord Rossington always had a care for his appearance, even when he could ill-afford to do so.'

'That has certainly changed now; he was determined that it should. Do you suppose he has brought his wife with him?'

'I *suppose* we shall find out very soon,' Louisa answered wryly.

Amy sat forward to instruct the driver to stop outside one of the Oxford Street emporiums she liked to patronise. 'We shall be an hour,' she told him as they stepped down. 'I must try to remember what I required to purchase,' she told Louisa. 'This untimely event has cast all else from my mind.'

'It is of no account,' her sister replied lightly, 'for I can remember every shop you wished to patronise.'

As they progressed along the busy shopping-street, the sisters encountered many people of their acquaintance. Those with whom they paused to converse did not mention Lord Rossington's return, and those who merely went by with a nod gave Louisa curious looks.

'Oh dear,' Louisa said at last. 'It seems

that no one wishes to comment upon the return of Lord Rossington. Don't you think that odd, Amy?'

Mrs. Mulcaster cast her a vexed look for making light of such a matter. 'Some people have consideration of your sensibilities, my dear.'

'That is odder still. However, if they are awaiting a display of my discomposure I regret they are bound for a disappointment.'

'You are a heartless creature,' her sister scolded.

Louisa grinned engagingly. 'Is it not Lord Rossington who is *that?*'

As they returned to the landau, Louisa succumbed to the temptation of buying some oranges from one of the many fruit-sellers who plied their trade along the street. She had just paid for her purchase when out of the corner of her eye she saw a particularly elegant phaeton bowling smartly down the road. Despite a proliferation of other traffic it seemed not to be held up at all.

When Mrs. Mulcaster saw who was driving it she drew in a sharp breath and looked towards a shop window in a deliberate gesture of dismissal. Louisa, however, could not help but admire such handsome equipage, and then, when she saw it was Lord Rossington who was tooling the ribbons, she would not look away. At his side was an exceedingly beautiful woman dressed in the height of fashion with many feathers in her wide-brimmed bonnet. They made a handsome pair, and Louisa was not the only one to note it. The progress of the phaeton was attracting a deal of interest.

As it drew level with Louisa, the earl caught sight of her. However, as on the previous evening there was no flicker of recognition on his face, and without a moment's hesitation he flicked his whip over the backs of the horses and drove on. The streets of London were always in a deplorable state, and as it passed the wheels of the phaeton flung up mud and water which splattered onto Louisa's skirt.

'Cor!' cried the orange-seller, 'them Quality ain't 'alf cockalorum wiv their fine carriages and the like. Now look at wot he done to yer duds.'

Louisa's mind was too full of what she had seen to take much note of the state of her clothes. 'I beg your pardon,' she said

46

to the pedlar, whose mode of speaking was unfamiliar to her.

'Oh, do look at you!' Mrs. Mulcaster cried. 'Your gown is quite ruined, I do declare.'

'Dora will soon clean it,' her sister answered calmly as Mrs. Mulcaster began to hurry her back to the carriage.

'The man has the audacity of a turkey cock.'

'Amy, he is perfectly at liberty to drive his carriage anywhere he pleases.'

'He should have the decency to stay away from you.'

'He couldn't possibly know...'

'Do you suppose that creature was his wife?'

'Possibly.'

'Men rarely take their wives riding. Most like she is a demirep.'

'A man might well take his wife riding if she was new to the country and wished to see a little of it before venturing out on her own.'

'That woman did not look in the least Russian.'

Louisa grinned at her disarmingly. 'The only Russian I have ever seen was in an illustration in a book I once read. He was a fierce creature dressed in bearskins, but I doubt if Lady Rossington would look like that, especially as Queen Catherine has rather an elegant court.'

Louisa was quite proud of making light of her sister's conversation. Amy would not be the only person of her acquaintance longing to make a Greek tragedy of the matter.

She climbed into the landau, and as she sank back into the squabs warned her sister. 'Amy, you may as well grow accustomed to seeing Lord Rossington at every turn. We mix in the same social circles, and your continual hand-wringing will serve only to delight the tattle-baskets.'

'You are quite splendid, Louisa. I am bound to admit that to you. I could not face this situation with such equanimity. Asquith, drive us home, if you please.' As she settled back in her seat she drew a deep sigh. 'I have been nought but a chucklehead over this. From now onwards I shall be as sophisticated as you.'

Louisa smiled slightly, feeling more than a little relieved, but not quite believing.

Mrs. Mulcaster's forecast, however, was correct. Lord Rossington was to be found at most of the functions Louisa attended. As diversions were normally held at the huge mansions of the *ton,* on most occasions she caught only a glimpse of him in the crowd, but once or twice mischief-making hostesses did attempt to thrust them together. The earl behaved at such times impeccably, exchanging with Louisa polite banalities before moving on as soon as politeness decreed it permissible. However much Louisa made light of the matter to her sister, she did nevertheless find those occasions fraught with tension. She felt she should respond to his questions with light, witty remarks, but only managed to feel awkward and as tongue-tied as a green girl.

Contrary to her instincts, Louisa did not shrink from such confrontations, fearing to give the gossips something to talk about. In fact she was seen abroad far more than hitherto, and certainly more often than she would have otherwise chosen.

She did not shrink from attending any ball, rout or drum, wholeheartedly partaking in parties at Vauxhall and Ranelagh, visited museums, the zoo and, most of all, rode regularly in the Park, although in truth she found such frenetic activity wearing and not as enjoyable as she pretended. It would have been far more to her fancy to walk in the country and spend her days quietly at the Mulcaster's home as she had on previous years.

Louisa continued in this fashion for several weeks, and at no time did anyone appear in the earl's company who might have been his wife, but although curiosity about her was rife, as a diplomat on a brief visit home it was assumed he had left her in St. Petersburg.

As a special treat for the two eldest Mulcaster girls, Louisa occasionally took them riding in the Park. All the paths were crowded, mostly with carriages of every description, but with horseriders and pedestrians too. The object was to see and be seen, and it mattered not a jot the means employed. The girls found it exciting, which caused Louisa to recall there was a time when she did so too.

'In two years' time you will be making your début,' Elizabeth said to her sister, her eyes bright with anticipation.

'I can scarce wait. When I have an establishment of my own, Aunt Louisa, shall you come and visit me?'

'I shall be hurt if you do not invite me.'

'And mine too!' Elizabeth said excitedly.

Louisa laughed. 'I shall not lack for agreeable accommodation in my old age.'

Joanna looked at her shyly then. 'Mayhap you will have an establishment of your own by then.'

'One can never tell,' Louisa answered non-committally.

She inclined her hand to a group of acquaintances who were strolling by and waved to Lady Fermoine who drove past in her own gig. Louisa was proud of her nieces and enjoyed being with them, but the speed with which they were growing into adults alarmed her as well as giving her pleasure.

When Sir Peter Fairchild came riding by on his hack Louisa ordered the carriage to stop and greeted him warmly.

'What a pleasure to espy not one, not two, but three beauties in one carriage,' he said. 'That vision must melt the heart of even the stoniest bachelor.'

'I trust you do not refer to yourself, Sir Peter,' Louisa retorted.

'Indeed not. I have always had a healthy respect for a pretty female.'

The two girls blushed, and Louisa said, 'Coming from anyone else, Sir Peter, I would take your words as flummery.'

'As indeed they would be. You all present a charming picture, but where is the fourth member of your family?'

'Mrs. Mulcaster had an appointment with her mantua-maker who is in great demand, so she dare not cry off even though she is vexed at missing her ride.'

'Quite understandable. Temperamental these seamstresses, especially the French ones.' He raised his hat. 'Until we meet again, ladies.'

He rode away, and Louisa was still smiling when she espied Lord Rossington riding towards them on his splendid black horse. Her smile faded somewhat, and she was about to instruct the driver to move on when she realised the earl was actually about to approach.

Ridiculously Louisa's heart began to beat fast.

'When I have my Season,' Joanna was telling her sister, 'my carriage will not be able to move more than a yard or two at a time for importuning young men.'

'During *my* come-out year,' her sister rejoined, 'I shall not be able to step outside the house without being beseiged.'

He was really too close to avoid, but

Louisa desperately affected not to have noticed him and leaned forward once more to instruct the driver.

'Good afternoon, Miss Farnham.'

Louisa sank back into the squabs. 'Good day, Lord Rossington,' she answered, without looking directly at him.

However, the girls were looking at him with interest, something for which their aunt could not blame them. He was quite out of the ordinary and was like to be noticed even in the densest crowd. If nothing else had done so, meeting him again had reinforced her belief that they had been ill-matched initially.

A few moments' silence followed his greeting, and when it became obvious he was not about to move on, Louisa was forced to say, 'Allow me to introduce my nieces, the Misses Joanna and Elizabeth Mulcaster. Girls, Lord Rossington.'

Joanna suddenly realised to whom she was being introduced and gasped, but had enough presence of mind to say, 'How do you do, my lord.'

Elizabeth pressed her hand to her lips to suppress a giggle, and Joanna was wavering between shock and amusement. The earl, however, displayed not the

53

slightest discomposure.

'Miss Joanna I remember well. You have certainly fulfilled your early promise of beauty.'

At this the girl could no longer stifle her giggles. Louisa, as was usual, could think of nothing more to say and hoped he would have the goodness to move on. Certainly the encounter was being keenly observed. People who had no cause to do so were dallying nearby, but at least it would not be said that Lord Rossington had snubbed her.

'I called earlier at Park Street,' he went on, much to Louisa's alarm. She looked at him at last, her eyes growing wide. 'Unfortunately no one was at home and I left my card.'

'We...have been out for some time,' she managed to reply.

He inclined his head slightly. 'I will call again at a more convenient time.'

Before she could say more, although she was quite at a loss for words, he rode on. The girls turned to watch him go, but Louisa immediately ordered the driver to take them home.

Joanna and Elizabeth were watching her in between casting each other wide-eyed looks. Louisa wondered what they expected her to do or say, and finally she turned to give them a wide smile.

'Your parents and I are attending the Devonshire's card-party this evening. Do you think I should wear the green Genoese velvet or the puce China silk? I cannot quite decide between them.'

Once again the girls exchanged wide-eyed looks, and then Elizabeth replied, 'Oh, it must be the Genoese velvet, Aunt Louisa. The colour becomes you well.'

Louisa drew a deep sigh and relaxed a little, but when she arrived back at her sister's house the girls went immediately upstairs to remove their bonnets and pelisses. When they were halfway up the stairs they could contain themselves no longer and began chattering in half whispers which did not hide their excitement.

Their aunt smiled indulgently, but immediately they were out of sight she began to sort through the cards which had been left in their absence. It was not something which she normally did, for so few callers were for her alone, nor was anyone of particular interest likely to call. There were several cards lying on a silver salver on one of the hall tables.

Louisa soon located Lord Rossington's. She gazed at it for a moment, wondering why he should choose to call at all. There was no cause for it, and should any of them have been at home to receive him only embarrassment would have ensued.

Oliver Mulcaster's house steward came into the hall, and Louisa immediately told him, 'Benton, will you let it be known to all the servants that if the Earl of Rossington calls none of us are in to him.'

'Certainly, madam.'

She drew in a deep breath, and then turned abruptly on her heel as Amy came bustling into the hall, pulling off her plumed hat and thrusting it into the hands of the waiting footman.

'So, you have just arrived home! Only wait until you see the gown I am going to wear tonight...'

Louisa smiled automatically at her sister as she surreptitiously slipped the calling-card into the muff she was still holding.

Amy slipped her arm into her sister's. 'Tell me, dearest, all whom you saw whilst you were out...'

'Just the usual faces, Amy,' she replied artlessly as they began to walk up the stairs together. 'Our ride was quite without incident.'

Four

It was several days later that Lord Rossington called again as he had promised. On this occasion Louisa and her sister were out making calls themselves, but Amy did see his card.

'My goodness! Only look who has called while we were out. The impudent puppy. Has he no consideration for your sensibilities?'

Louisa took the card from her hand and tore it into pieces before dropping it back onto the tray.

'I believe he has great regard for my sensibilities, my dear, so you need not be in such a taking. However, I have already given instructions for him not to be admitted.'

Her sister looked both surprised and pleased. 'Would that he were so sensible.

I do wish,' she added with a sigh, 'he hadn't chosen this precise time to return to England. It is most annoying to find him present everywhere we go.'

Louisa had no wish to get into a conversation about Lord Rossington's shortcomings and began to walk up the stairs. 'Quite conversely, Amy dear, he might consider it vexing to find *us* wherever he goes.'

There came no answer, but when Louisa looked back with a smile her sister was staring at her in amazement.

Despite her calm stance in front of Amy, Louisa knew he would call again, and she did not relish the thought. If he regarded a formal call right and proper that was what he would achieve. She only hoped she could contrive to be out whenever he came, for beyond the few basic politenesses they had already exchanged she had no notion what to say to him. It had often been so in the brief period of their betrothal. Then as now, Louisa had been slightly overawed by him, even though now she was older she was certainly more in command of herself.

When he did not come again Louisa began to relax more, believing perhaps he considered his duty discharged by the two previous calls. She certainly hoped so.

However, he did come again, this time when Louisa was at home. In fact she was just about to come downstairs with her nephew when the earl strode into the hall, causing her to draw back abruptly into the shadows.

She could see him quite clearly from the landing, dressed in a caped driving-coat and beaver hat. Not for the first time did she reflect the intervening years had bestowed upon him a sense of style and presence he hadn't possessed before.

'Go back upstairs,' she whispered to the boy, 'and I will fetch you presently.'

As the child went away Louisa heard the footman saying, 'I regret that Mr. and Mrs. Mulcaster are not at home.'

'That is unfortunate, but perhaps Miss Farnham will receive me in their stead.'

'I regret, my lord...'

He was looking around him and obviously irritated, which was indicated by the way he was slapping his riding-whip against his gloved palm. Suddenly he caught sight of Louisa hovering uncertainly at the top of the stairs, and he strode purposefully across the hall.

'Miss Farnham, will you receive me for a few moments?'

Louisa looked past him to the footman. 'When will Mrs. Mulcaster return?'

'She didn't say, ma'am. She received a note this morning after breakfast and went out immediately.'

'You can leave the door open if you so wish,' the earl called up to her.

Irritated by his sarcasm, she told the footman, 'Grives, show his lordship to the drawing-room.'

Before he was ushered into her presence Louisa paused to ascertain that every hair was in place and rubbed her cheeks to inject them with colour. Adjusting the lace tucker at her bosom she hurried into the drawing-room to await the caller.

She was composed by the time he was ushered into the drawing-room. The servant had relieved him of his greatcoat, hat, gloves and whip, and he was wearing a sober coat of dark cloth which fitted well.

Louisa stood inside the room, her hands clasped in front of her, a stance which belied her uncertain feelings. Polite conversation with this man would be totally out of place.

When the footman had withdrawn she

said, 'Won't you please be seated, Lord Rossington?'

'After you, ma'am.'

She sat down on the edge of a satin-covered sofa and was relieved when he chose a chair near the fire some distance away.

'It was good of you to receive me, Miss Farnham.'

'You must understand I am not in the habit of receiving gentlemen visitors in my sister's absence, Lord Rossington.'

'I am fully aware of that, so I must confess without delay that I chose a moment when I knew both Mr. and Mrs. Mulcaster would not be at home.' Louisa stiffened, sitting up even straighter in the chair. He smiled slightly, something she had not often seen. 'If we are to speak with any degree of ease, Miss Farnham, I deemed it prudent that it should be without a few hundred others being witness to it.'

She relaxed only slightly. To be at ease with him was impossible. 'Your solicitude in that respect does you credit, but in truth, Lord Rossington, your concern is without foundation.'

'You must own that we cannot converse

in public because of the interest it would invoke.'

'That is so, but I cannot conceive what we might have to say to each other.'

'Indeed not, but I had hoped the passage of so many years since we last met might have rendered the past into the realms of history.'

Louisa looked away. 'Be assured I have no feelings of any kind on the matter.'

'That, Miss Farnham, is a great relief to me.' After a moment's silence he added in a softer voice, 'You look very well.'

Her hands twisted convulsively in her lap. 'I am in tolerable health, I thank you.'

''Tis amazing you look no older than on the last occasion that we met. That was at Lady Vaseney's ball, was is not?'

Her eyes remained downcast, and she hoped he would not note the colour spreading up her cheeks. 'You have an excellent memory.'

'None better,' he admitted, lifting a snuff-box from his pocket and taking a pinch.

Unable to remain still a moment longer and wishing Amy would return Louisa got to her feet.

'May I offer you refreshment, Lord Rossington?'

She went towards the bell-pull, glad of something to do, but he put up his hand. 'No, I thank you, ma'am. As I promised I will not detain you much longer.'

Reluctantly, Louisa returned to her seat, relieved at least that he intended to go quite soon, for his visit was far more of an ordeal than she would have imagined.

'Is your wife with you in London?' she asked, knowing full well she was not otherwise the news would be known by now, but the query did bridge an awkward silence and she did feel it was necessary to ask.

In the event Louisa was sorry she did ask, for he replied, 'My wife died six months ago.'

Louisa looked stricken, and did feel the blow deeply. 'Oh, I am indeed sorry to hear you say so, Lord Rossington. How dreadful for you. Was it a sudden occurrence?'

'Alas yes.' As his manner was normally undemonstrative Louisa should not have been surprised at the detached way he spoke of such tragedy, but she was. 'That was one reason why I decided to return to England at last.'

'Such sadness, 'tis no wonder.'

'I deemed it prudent to bring our son to England at this time.'

She had not, somehow, envisaged a child, and was, despite everything, shocked by the revelation. 'I had no notion...'

The earl smiled again. 'Nicholas is at Trevarrick with his nursemaid. He has not been quite well since his mother died, so I considered it best to allow him to remain in Cornwall for the time being.'

Having quickly recovered from her dismay, she answered, 'Very wise of you, Lord Rossington. The country air is most beneficial, and I am told Cornish air particularly so.'

It suddenly occurred to Louisa how ludicrous this polite conversation was becoming between two who were once promised to each other, and for the first time she realised that if circumstances and fate had decreed, she would have been a married lady of nine years' standing, no doubt with a nursery full of children of her own. The notion caused her cheeks to redden, and a silence once again ensued until the earl, apparently unaware of her confusion of mind, spoke again.

'I must confess that I was surprised to find you still unwed, Miss Farnham.'

She knew he was looking at her speculatively, and she kept her eyes downcast.

'I...decided not to marry,' she answered at last.

He got to his feet and she looked up sharply, hoping that he would at last leave, but he merely moved to stand in front of the fireplace, his hands clasped behind his back.

He seemed to tower over her, and the fact that he was regarding her intensely made her look away again.

'Miss Farnham...Louisa...' She almost flinched at his use of her name, 'I shall not mince words with you any longer. I came here with a purpose which has been in my mind for several weeks, although now we are face to face I find speaking out inordinately difficult in view of what has gone before.'

Slowly she raised her eyes to cast him a curious look and her heart began to thump noisily, for she feared he would wish to talk about the past and that was something she did not wish to do.

For once he could not meet her questioning gaze. 'The truth is I need assistance in a matter dear to me, and it has become increasingly obvious to me that you are the only person to whom I can apply.'

Louisa's hand fluttered uncertainly around her trembling lips. 'I...Lord Rossington?'

'You once called me Rohan.'

She turned away, and he went on quickly. 'That was unpardonable of me. Please forgive me.'

'There is nothing to forgive,' she answered, swallowing quickly. 'I believe you were entreating my help on some matter.'

He seemed somewhat relieved. 'With Nicholas.'

'Your son!'

'Past knowledge of you, and from all I have observed and heard of late, leads me to believe you can help with him.'

'What manner of help, Lord Rossington?'

'Ah, that is the problem. He is difficult, Miss Farnham, and I confess I am at a loss how to deal with him.' Louisa cast him a look of blatant disbelief, and he went on, 'For example, he refuses to speak English although he can do so with ease, and in this he is encouraged by his nurse. I wish to send her back to St. Petersburg, but I cannot until there is someone to whom I can entrust his upbringing. None of my servants are willing or able to do it.'

'But how can I possibly help? If he is at Trevarrick you need to engage a governess, and that should not be a difficult task. If you wish me to engage one on your behalf I will certainly do so.'

He shook his head. 'That will not do, I fear. No governess has so far been able to cope with such a disobedient and difficult child.'

She cast him a scornful look. 'No child can be so impossible, but I am at a loss what to suggest to you. I still believe a gov...'

'You are the only person who could possibly do all that is necessary to turn him into a responsible English gentleman.'

Louisa got to her feet, clasping her hands in front of her and laughing uneasily. 'Oh, Lord Rossington, you flatter me far too much, and even if I were willing to come to Trevarrick in such a capacity—a governess of sorts, I suppose—my brother-in-law would not hear of it.'

She turned away so he could not see her discomposure. Her thoughts were quite incoherent, not knowing what to make of his proposal.

'I would not expect him to, nor would I make such an offer to you—of all people. Nicholas does not need a governess, as I have already said. He needs a mother. Of all men I have the least right to ask this of you, but will you marry me, Louisa?'

Now she turned on her heel, her eyes wide, her breast heaving beneath the fine gauze fichu. She stared at him in astonishment, unable to speak, shocked and alarmed at so unexpected a pronouncement.

'I realise that you did not look for this offer, nor am I making it in the normal way, you understand.' He stood ramrod straight, looking directly ahead of him, his hands clasped composedly behind his back. 'The marriage would be on your terms, naturally. We cannot pretend to ourselves that it is anything other than a convenience.'

'To you indeed.'

He continued to stare straight ahead of him. 'In return for your being a mother to my son, you shall have my name and an establishment of your own with the addition of a generous allowance of pin-money, which must be an asset to a woman such as you.'

Louisa stiffened angrily. 'An old maid, you mean, Lord Rossington.'

'No,' he answered in a softer voice, looking at her at last. 'A woman of taste and great sensibility. In purely material terms I have a good deal to offer and I ask only in exchange your care of my son.'

Her eyebrows rose a fraction, and he went on, taking a pinch of snuff to cover up, she was certain, his own uncharacteristic discomposure, 'The house, too, will be in your charge, if that is what you wish, but I vow I shall ask no more of you. I believe you would find it a congenial arrangement. You would see little of me. Later, if you wish and when Nicholas is older, we can spend time in London which will enable you to become a Society hostess. You will be able to entertain as lavishly as you please. I ask only that you devote yourself to Nicholas for a while.'

'That is all?' she asked unsteadily.

His eyes met her once again. 'Yes, that is all.'

She drew in a deep breath before saying. 'You have been exceedingly frank, Lord Rossington, but this offer has come as a great surprise. Nine years ago when our betrothal was ended...'

'You must not think of it, and neither shall I. Neither of us are the people we were then. Circumstances and time have changed us.'

He held her gaze yet again, and it seemed that time stood still. Louisa wasn't even sure either of them breathed for the few moments it lasted, and then both doors to the drawing-room flew open and Mrs. Mulcaster came hurrying in. Her face bore an unusually steely look for a lady who was even-tempered.

'Lord Rossington, I certainly did not look to see you here.'

'I trust you will forgive the intrusion,' he answered, turning on his heel to face her.

He took her hand and raised it to his lips whilst she cast Louisa a questioning look over his shoulder. However, she could not have known exactly what had caused such an agonised look on her sister's face.

Stepping back, he said. 'I shall not detain you ladies any longer.' And then, glancing at Louisa, he added in a soft voice, 'I appreciate that you need time to consider, but I needs must return to Trevarrick within the month.'

Amy watched him go with eyes as cold as ice before she cried to her sister, 'Would that I could have been here when he arrived! He would not have been allowed within half a mile of you.'

'It is of no account, Amy,' Louisa answered in a muted tone, walking towards the window.

Gazing down in the street, she could see the earl's curricle, his horses waiting restively for his return.

'Dear Arabella began her travail this morning, and as soon as I received her note I had to rush to her side. Another daughter—however, she is not downcast, I confess. There is always next year.'

She moved towards her sister who was still deep in thought. 'What has that scoundrel said to you? Oh, if only I could have prevented his coming. It shall not happen again, you may be quite certain, my dear.'

71

'Pray do not get into a pucker over this, Amy.'

The earl was making his departure. She watched him climb into the curricle and take the ribbons. As he did so he paused to look up to where she was standing at the window as if he knew she would be there, and he raised his hat. Louisa quickly moved away again, and Mrs. Mulcaster's eyes narrowed suddenly.

'What is it that you have to consider?'

She could see no point in prevaricating. 'Lord Rossington has made me an offer of marriage.'

Mrs. Mulcaster stepped back as if she had been slapped. 'You are surely gammoning me?'

'Indeed, I am not.'

'But he is already wed.'

'His wife has died, Amy.'

Amy's face crumpled into a mask of fury. 'Oh, the heartless poltroon. Does he seek to make good now his treatment of you? When Mr. Mulcaster is told of this he is certain to call him out. I trust you sent him away with a flea in his ear.'

'Don't be a goosecap, Amy. It was a perfectly genuine offer and I cannot credit your dismay. You wish me to be wed, do you not?'

'Naturally, but...'

'Even you did not dare to hope for such a brilliant match.'

'Not Lord Rossington!' Amy gasped. 'He has caused you enough unhappiness already.'

'The circumstances in which that applied no longer exist. Here is a man of importance, Amy. His fortunes have been reversed and his appearance certainly is pleasing. How can one wish for more?'

Louisa began to walk towards the door.

'You surely do not intend to consider it,' her sister called after her.

She smiled and replied, 'I would be a chucklehead if I did not, Amy. Pray excuse me. Before Lord Rossington arrived I promised Julian I would play shuttlecock with him in the garden. He will be waiting impatiently by now.'

Louisa left her sister with her mouth agape, but as soon as she had left the room her composure began to fade. She started to shiver, and it was some time before she felt sufficiently composed to play shuttlecock with her nephew after all.

Five

The yacht *Natalia* cleaved its way through the uneven waters of the English channel towards the Cornish peninsula. The voyage, although not a long one, had not been too smooth and Louisa, being unused to sea travelling, had been ill for a while. The voyage from London to Trevarrick had been, in the eyes of the world, a romantic wedding-trip for the Earl and new Countess of Rossington now that Napoleon Bonaparte had rendered Europe unsafe for travellers.

Louisa could not help but smile whenever she recalled how romantic her wedding appeared to the *ton,* taking place nine years after it should have done. A fairy tale ending to a sad story, for no one, apart from the earl and herself, knew the true status of their marriage.

Louisa had agreed to enter a loveless marriage without considering the consequences too deeply. Only after the splendid wedding-feast—when so many envious eyes were upon her—and their subsequent embarkation, did she feel uneasy about so unnatural state of affairs, for it was obvious his first marriage had been a normal one. However, the earl displayed no such unease and, true to his word, had not come to her cabin for any reason. It was, perhaps, just as well, for she had been ill for most of the time. When she was well enough, they met only on deck or in the dining-room, but that had not been too often.

Despite memories of her sister's tearful face as they bade each other good-bye after a wedding attended by everyone of any consequence, Louisa did not regret her decision to marry the earl. No longer could she be regarded as Poor Aunt Louisa, but the Countess of Rossington, a lady of great consequence. After her brief incursion into the social round, Louisa had been left in no doubt about the advantages of that.

She would miss Amy and Oliver, and the children, of course, but they had promised to visit Trevarrick in the summer. Louisa supposed the earl would not mind, and she was certain Amy would come, if only to make sure Louisa was not being ill-treated by her new husband. The thought made her smile; he would not mistreat her, for he scarce heeded her at all.

The boat gently rolled and there came a knock on the door. Louisa sat up in the bed which was swathed by scarlet velvet and gold tassels. Her entire cabin was extravagantly furnished, presumably by the late countess. It was not to Louisa's taste so she was glad she did not have to live there.

The cabin door opened and Louisa's maid, looking pale and ill, stepped inside.

'I thought you were resting, Dora?'

'So I was, ma'am, but his lordship wanted me to tell you he'd like you to join him on deck, if you're feeling up to it.'

Louisa slipped her feet over the side of the bed. 'Tidy my hair, Dora, and then you may go and lie down again.'

The girl's deft fingers began to put Louisa's hair into its formerly smooth style. 'Don't like this sea voyaging, ma'am, and that's the truth,' she complained as she worked.

'It's just as well we'll soon reach land.'

'Can't be soon enough for me, ma'am. Never felt so ill in my life. Thought I was dying that first night, I did.'

Louisa recalled the feeling well, moreover the chagrin that her husband should witness it. 'Just imagine what it must have been like to sail all the way from St. Petersburg to England as Lord Rossington did.'

'Don't say we're having to go there too, ma'am.'

Louisa laughed at her concern. 'No, Dora. Lord Rossington has resigned his diplomatic post and we shall settle at Trevarrick.'

'I'm glad to hear it, ma'am. Cornwall's far enough for me. Treat newcomers like foreigners, I'm told. Strange place, strange folk.'

'Recall that we shall still be in England, Dora,' Louisa pointed out wryly.

'Not so you'd believe it, ma'am.'

When her hair was tidy Louisa put on her warmest pelisse and left the cabin, making her way slowly up to the deck. The earl was standing on the poop, looking shoreward through a glass. To Louisa's relief the sea was much calmer and the craggy coastline in view at last.

When he became aware of her unsteady step on the deck he put down the glass and turned to her. 'Are you feeling better?' he asked, his tone characteristically cool.

77

'Yes, I thank you.'

'I am pleased to hear it. A few minutes on deck should help to restore the colour to your cheeks.'

Louisa automatically put her hands up to them. 'Dora has put some rouge on them, but do I look so bad?'

'You look much better than you did two days ago.'

She smiled faintly. 'How tiresome you must find me.'

'Not at all. So many people find sea travel distressing. I should have asked your preference, but because the yacht was moored on the Thames it was a better mode of transport than by carriage.'

'And so it is. Much better than frequent horse changes and putting up at inferior hostelries. This mode of travel is quite a novelty to me and I promise you next time I shall be perfectly well.'

'Yes, I'm persuaded that you will.'

When she transferred her attention to him she thought he was looking at her admiringly and said quickly, to cover her confusion, 'Are we near our destination yet?'

'See for yourself.'

He handed her the glass, and she put

78

it to her eye. It took her a moment or two to focus on the shore, but when she did she could see only rocky inlets and bare cliffs.

'Can I see the house itself?' she asked, and his answer was to turn her round until the house was in view.

Louisa gasped at the sight of the great grey stone house on top of a bluff which overlooked a creek. She had always harboured a curiosity about Trevarrick, for twenty years earlier the earl's father had ruined himself building the house, and he and his wife had travelled the length and breadth of Europe seeking art treasures and furnishings to lavish on his mansion. It was these events which had forced their son to seek a wealthy bride to mend the family fortunes.

'What do you think?' he asked at last, and she was suddenly and uncomfortably aware he still held her.

'It's...splendid. Quite splendid.'

'Not worth the cost, however,' he answered wryly, and Louisa put the glass down at last, causing his hands to fall from her shoulders.

He stepped back a pace as if he too had only just become aware of their close proximity to each other. 'It is prodigiously shabby after so many years of neglect. When you are able, you can attend to such matters.' And then, as if reading her mind, he added, sounding slightly discomforted, 'My first wife never came to England. She never lived in Trevarrick.'

'Yes,' she breathed, and could only be thankful there would be no reminders here of the exotic princess he had loved and lost, which struck her as being odd in view of their businesslike arrangement.

A moment later she smiled. 'You will not find me extravagant in such matters.'

He smiled too, which was rare. In fact, it was only rarely that they were able to speak together with such accord.

'I am fully aware of that.'

Embarrassed by his gentleness, Louisa said, more briskly, 'When are we due to arrive?'

'Within the hour if the tide continues to run briskly.'

'In that event, with your permission, I shall prepare to go ashore.'

'Of course.'

She began to pick her way across the deck once again, unaware that he was watching her until he called her name and she turned to him. His hair was blowing in the wind and his expression was strangely enigmatic, and for a moment she experienced an emotion she could not recognise. All she knew was that it was previously unknown to her.

As she looked at him questioningly, he said, 'I truly hope you will be happy here.'

'I cannot conceive why I should not,' she answered in a strangled voice.

'You have not met the child as yet.'

'I look forward to that with eagerness, for I cannot credit he is as difficult as you say. Even so the terms of our agreement are hardly onerous to me.'

He stared at her hard. 'I take it that our agreement is still to your satisfaction, Louisa.'

She stiffened slightly as a gust of wind temporarily buffeted her off-balance. Her husband was immediately at her side to steady her and when she straightened up she gripped onto a rail rather than onto him.

'Our agreement,' she said breathlessly.

'It was foolish of me to mention it,' he conceded as he relinquished his hold on her. 'Go now to your cabin. I will call you when we're ready to go ashore.'

At last she drew further away from him and, gathering up her skirts, she hurried below at last.

A score of servants were standing by the jetty when the yacht tied up in the creek. Louisa deliberately remained in her cabin until one of the crew summoned her on deck. Only then did she venture into the open again.

The earl was the first ashore, and he immediately gave his hand to his wife. A carriage had been brought down from the house so that the new countess was not obliged to brave the cold wind a moment longer than was necessary. The cold wind was, in fact, the least of her concerns.

Although she was delighted to be on firm land at last that pleasure was somewhat dissipated by the fact she had behaved like a frightened rabbit when her husband had only expressed concern for her. Her cheeks flushed at the memory, but fortuitously the earl was far too busy to notice. Servants were scurrying everywhere, unloading baggage into carts. After a few moments the carriage springs groaned as the earl climbed in and they set off towards Trevarrick at last.

He sank into the seat facing hers and gave her a reassuring smile, although it was a cold and distant one on this occasion, she noted.

'A few minutes only and we shall be there.'

Suddenly Louisa was assailed with panic. Never before had she doubted she would not be equal to the task before her, but now she wondered how easy it would be to run a house where the order had been unchanged for years. Somehow she suspected her husband would not often be there to assist. He would expect to be left to his own pursuits.

The path to the house wound upwards, and at the turn of one bend Trevarrick loomed in front of her, its mullions alight as they reflected the dying winter sun. It was like a grey stone monster with eyes of fire. Past another bend and the illusion faded although the house was indeed larger than it appeared from the sea.

The earl seemed unaware of her apprehension as the carriage came to a halt outside the porticoed main entrance. The door was open to reveal lights already kindled within, and Louisa could see the glow of a fire in the hearth. That in itself seemed welcoming.

A footman let down the steps and the earl climbed down. Louisa hesitated a little before taking his proferred hand. He looked up at her and she sought vainly for something to say to him, but no words would come, and she climbed down, feeling foolish although not knowing why. He relinquished his grip on her hand as soon as she had stepped down, and the lack of any warmth or affection between them was telling now. Arriving at her new home as mistress of the house, Louisa desperately needed his support of her. In a normal marriage a woman might take such support for granted, but she was miserably alone and never more aware of it than now.

'The servants are lined up, ready for you, my Lord,' announced the man who was obviously the house-steward, resplendent in the gold and green livery worn by all the other male servants too.

'Thank you, Jenkins,' the earl replied, and Louisa suddenly hated him for being at home here when she was quite certain she could never be that. 'Allow me to present the countess.'

The man bowed low and said, 'Welcome to Trevarrick, my lady.'

'Thank you, Jenkins,' Louisa answered, injecting some warmth into her voice, despite her secret feelings. 'I am very pleased to be here.'

'Will you come this way, my lady?'

She glanced at her husband who was watching her quietly, and after hesitating only a moment followed the house-steward indoors.

A prodigious number of servants were assembled in the hall for presentation to their new mistress. After the house-steward, the most important servant was the housekeeper, a short, stout lady who was dressed entirely in black bombazine. After the housekeeper had presented Louisa ceremoniously with a large bunch of keys, Jenkins presented a number of servants in diminishing importance whilst the earl studied various documents which had arrived in his absence.

Last to be introduced was a gentleman quietly waiting at the end of the line.

'This, my dear, is Mr. Mark Logan, my land-steward, who manages my estate with such good results,' the earl said, returning his attention to her at last.

The fair-haired young man bowed low over her hand in response to the introduction. 'This is indeed a great honour, my lady.'

'I am very pleased to make the acquaintance of someone who stands so highly in my husband's regard, Mr. Logan.'

The man straightened up, regarding her with deep blue eyes in a way which was not unflattering. Louisa immediately felt he would be a friend, and the notion pleased her.

'I can only hope in the time to come you will also come to look upon me in a similar way, ma'am, for I intend to be of service to you also.'

His look was one of undisguised admiration, which did not go amiss; and now the ordeal of arriving and meeting the servants was over Louisa was beginning to feel much happier. They all looked at her with such awe, which was quite a change.

'Logan,' said the earl, 'you must join us for dinner tonight and we can talk at length afterwards.'

The young man was obviously taken aback at being asked to join a newly wed couple their first night home, but he quickly recovered his composure.

'It will be a pleasure, my lord.' He glanced at Louisa, bowing again. 'If you will excuse me.'

'May I dismiss the servants, my lady?' Jenkins asked as soon as the land-steward had gone.

'Oh, please do, Jenkins. How remiss of me.'

She drew off her gloves and glanced around her at last. The hall had an almost medieval splendour. A flight of stone steps reached upwards to a wide gallery where suits of armour stood to attention watched over by rows of sombre portraits of long-dead Rossingtons.

All round her the servants, who had broken ranks, were going about their respective duties except for Jenkins and Mrs. Pendas the housekeeper, and it was to her that the earl addressed himself next.

'Has Viscount Danby been informed of our arrival?'

'Yes, my lord. The Russian...his nurse-maid was told to make him ready.'

A look of irritation crossed the earl's face, but no sooner had the housekeeper spoken than a commotion on the landing caused them all to look up. An elderly woman was pulling a small child along the landing whilst he resisted all her efforts as he screamed and shouted in French.

'*Au secours! Laissez-moi tranquille! Zut! Idiot!*'

'Nicholas!'

The woman was almost carrying the child, but at the sound of his father's furious voice he halted his harangue.

'Stop this disgraceful behaviour and come downstairs immediately.'

He did so, but reluctantly, followed by his nurse who stared hard at Louisa with undisguised hostility. Louisa was scarcely aware of her; her eyes were on the child who was wearing a shirt and breeches, which looked as if they had been hurriedly donned for he was less than neat. His eyes were fixed on his father, his dark hair tousled. Louisa was pleased and a little relieved to note that he strongly resembled the earl.

'Come and pay your respects to my new wife; your step-mother, Nicholas.'

The boy stared mutinously at her then and his father prompted, 'Well, what do you say?'

'Nikolai,' cried the nursemaid, something which caused the earl to turn on her furiously.

'Woman, did I not forbid you to call him that?'

Louisa was beginning to feel distinctly discomforted as the child continued to stare at his father defiantly. She realised that this was one confrontation the earl was bound to lose, and it was odd to see him so out of control of the situation.

The woman lowered her eyes, murmuring her apologies, but her expression remain defiant.

'Now, Nicholas,' his father began, transferring his attention to the boy again, 'I am fast losing patience with you.'

'I will not call her Mama!' the boy cried in English at last.

'You don't have to call me Mama,' Louisa assured him in a soothing voice. 'Call me Aunt Louisa.'

If she had hoped to take some tension out of the situation she failed, for the child cried, shrilly 'No! I hate you!' and turned on his heel, running back towards his nurse.

He did not reach her, for the earl leaped forward and caught him round the waist. Louisa watched, fearful of interfering at this early stage and yet knowing her husband was dealing with the situation wrongly.

He carried the screaming boy to a chair, and snatching a riding-whip from one of the tables turned him over and began to bring it down on the child's bottom.

Louisa did act then, rushing over to them, adding her own cries to those of the child.

'Oh, do stop it!' she begged. 'Stop it, I say!'

Later she was to reflect what an odd scene it must have presented to onlookers, with the master, mistress and young heir in an undignified tangle. Somewhat to her surprise the earl let the child go, and he ran without a pause to his nurse who clasped him to her before hurrying him up the stairs.

The earl jumped to his feet, pulling at his coat which had become crumpled during the struggle. His furious stare followed the retreating pair, and then he said in a voice which was hoarse with fury, 'Mrs. Pendas, he is to have no supper tonight.'

'Yes, my lord,' came the answer, not without some satisfaction, which told

Louisa the child had not given his father's servants an easy time in his absence.

When his son had gone the earl gave Louisa a brief, cold look and added, 'Mrs. Pendas, show her ladyship to her room.'

He turned away, and Louisa said, 'Not yet. We must talk about this.'

'Later,' he answered abruptly without looking at her.

He went into one of the rooms which led off the hall, leaving Louisa alone with the servants. After a moment or two she turned to force a smile at the housekeeper.

'I would like to see my rooms now, Mrs. Pendas, if you please.'

The woman inclined her head and, still clutching the keys of the house, Louisa started up the stairs.

Six

Louisa reflected that she had been a fool to think the task would be an easy one. Someone as astute as the Earl of Rossington would not take a woman as his wife when some other solution was more readily available. He had asked her out of desperation, she could see that now, and if the title of Countess of Rossington was to be her reward she would earn it dearly.

Mrs. Pendas led the way down long, panelled corridors lined with murky portraits. The floors, Louisa noted, were well polished, and the odour of beeswax was so strong that a good deal of preparation had been made for her arrival.

When at last they came to the master-suite, the woman ushered her into a spacious bedchamber where Dora was already at work unpacking all the trunks which had been taken off the yacht. An evening-gown of pale yellow muslin was set out on the bed.

Louisa was relieved to discover her room so pleasantly appointed, filled with pieces of elegant French furniture which she guessed were collected by the earl's late mother, who was herself French.

'The room is unchanged since the late countess occupied it, my lady,' the housekeeper explained almost apologetically, as Louisa glanced quickly around her.

'It's charming,' she answered, truthfully. 'She must have been a lady of excellent taste.'

The housekeeper smiled for the first time. 'She was, my lady. If there is anything else you require, please ring.'

Just then one of the maidservants Louisa had seen downstairs entered the room, bearing a large pitcher of hot water. Louisa threw down her muff, saying, 'Mrs. Pendas, it is obvious to me everything I could possibly require is already here.'

The woman seemed gratified. 'No doubt your ladyship will wish to make changes to suit yourself.'

'You have run the house excellently in Lord Rossington's absence, and I trust you will continue to do so in much the same way.' From the woman's expression it was clear Louisa had said the correct thing. 'Naturally, I will suggest improvements from time to time, and there will be some refurnishing in due course, but I will be honest with you, Mrs. Pendas, I regard my first task to forge some relationship with Viscount Danby.'

The woman's face went tight. 'If I may take the liberty of saying so, my lady, you will not find that an easy task.'

'Indeed not, Mrs. Pendas. I shall need all the help and support that is possible, and that is why I am returning these keys to you. Until I have more time to attend household duties will you retain these? It would be onerous to both of us if you were obliged to seek me out whenever you wanted access to the linen cupboard or the stillroom.'

The housekeeper flushed with pleasure. 'If it is your wish, my lady. Just let me know your orders, ma'am, and they'll be carried out immediately. Tomorrow, if it suits you, I will show you around the house.'

'Thank you, Mrs. Pendas, I would like that. After breakfast perhaps.'

The woman bobbed a curtsy, and as she reached the door she paused to glance at Louisa again. 'It's good to have a mistress in the house again, ma'am.'

When she had gone Louisa turned to look about her in more detail, and Dora said, 'She was well nigh greasing your boots, ma'am.'

Louisa smiled. 'Gaining the housekeeper's goodwill is very important, Dora.' She opened an elaborately carved press to find many of her gowns already inside. 'Gaining Mrs. Pendas's goodwill is the easiest of my problems to solve, I fear.'

'The little boy, you mean. A terrible

to-do. I could hear it from here.'

One of the doors led to a small dressing-room, the other she discovered to another bedroom. It was furnished in a similar fashion to her own, with the addition of a gentleman's shaving-table. A wig-stand was on the dressing-table, but no man of fashion wore one since the tax on powder had risen so steeply.

The earl's valet was busily putting out his master's evening-clothes, and as Louisa came into the room he paused long enough to bow to her.

'May I be of assistance, my lady?'

'No, I thank you.' She backed away. 'I was merely finding my way.'

As she was just about to return to her own room the earl came striding in. He stopped abruptly when he saw her there, causing Louisa to flush with embarrassment.

'Louisa?' he enquired, twisting the diamond ring on his little finger around in an absent fashion.

'I was merely exploring my new surroundings. I hope you do not mind the intrusion.'

'Of course not. I trust the apartment is to your satisfaction.'

'Yes,' she breathed. 'I am well pleased with it. May I have words with you after dinner?'

'Before dinner I think would be better. It is necessary for me to speak with Logan afterwards.'

Louisa nodded, and after a moment she returned to her own room. As she closed the door she noticed then that there was a key in the lock. It had been unlocked initially, and she had no intention of turning the key on her side of the door.

Dora came to unhook her gown. 'The house is ever so big, bigger, I'm thinking, than Levenham.'

'Much,' Louisa answered absently, wondering if it was going to be as simple as it had seemed to be married to this man. It had all seemed so straightforward in London, but now doubts were beginning to creep in.

'There's a fine view from the window by day, ma'am, right across the grounds to the creek.'

'I'm persuaded life here will be pleasant for all of us,' Louisa told her, and although this seemed to reassure the maid, the new countess was far less certain.

A footman holding a branch of candles lighted her way down the curving staircase an hour later. If, inwardly, Louisa felt afraid and uncertain, her outward appearance gave no sign of it.

The servant threw open a door and ushered her into a small library where a fire burned welcomingly in the hearth. The earl, having changed his clothes too, was in the process of pouring a drink for himself. He looked up from the task as she entered the room. The servant withdrew, and Louisa came further into the room.

The candles in wall-sconces cast a flickering light over the bookshelves, giving the room a cosy glow. The heavy velvet curtains were now drawn against the night, but beyond them the sea would be creaming against the rocks. A strange place, hardly English, she thought. It was no wonder the sons of Cornwall were such an alien breed.

'You look very charming, my dear,' he said, and although she was faintly pleased by his praise she was also aware he was not really interested in her appearance and the comment was a mandatory one.

'Thank you,' she murmured, none the less.

He ushered her to a chair near the fire before asking, 'Would you like a glass of madeira? Ratafia perhaps?'

'No, I thank you. Nothing.'

He peered at her then. 'You are still not feeling well, I think.'

She smiled faintly then. 'I am perfectly well.'

'You relieve me.' After a moment's silence during which Louisa sat with her hands folded and her eyes downcast, he said, 'A year ago I never dreamed I would bring you here.'

'A month ago I would have been hard pressed to believe it too. It seems it was meant to be after all.'

A silence descended upon them once again before he took out his gold hunter. Drawing his gaze from her at last he glanced at it before putting it away again. 'I regret having to neglect you on our first night at Trevarrick, Louisa, but my discussion with Logan will not wait.'

'I understand perfectly. You must not feel you're neglecting me when you attend your business. I shall be well occupied with matters of my own, you may be sure.'

'So I supposed,' he answered, moving away and seating himself on the edge of the desk. 'However, we do have time for a coze now. In the days to come you must make an inventory of the improvements you'd like to see...'

'There will be time for that later. Most pressing is what is to be done about the child.'

He sighed and lifted his glass to his lips. 'Ah yes, the child.'

She raised her eyes at last. 'You brought me here to take charge of your son, so I may as well tell you from the outset I will not tolerate him being horse-whipped whatever the provocation.'

He sighed again. 'Do you think I make a habit of doing so?' She looked away, and he said, irritably, 'Well, do you?'

'Of course not,' she answered shortly.

'I was angered beyond reason by his behaviour. If nothing else I wanted your first meeting with him to be an affable one.'

'That was unusually unrealistic of you. You must not be too harsh on him. He is so very young, and only think what he has endured of late; losing his mother and being brought to a country which is quite alien to him. Oh, and pray do not be so angry when he speaks in French, for he may only do so to see that effect in you. Merely speak to him in English all the time and he will soon grow weary of trying to rouse you to anger.'

He smiled slightly as he reached out to refill the glass. 'I see he has an ally in you already, although after the way he behaved...'

She waved her hand in the air. 'It was only to be expected.'

'Now you are here I must make arrangements to send Anouska back to St. Petersburg. She is not a good influence on him, and of course she is too old. She was Natalia's nursemaid when she was a child. Because she was given entire charge of her she thinks she should enjoy the same privilege with Nicholas, but it will not do.'

'I am in agreement with you, but I beg of you do not dismiss her just yet. It is far too soon, coming hard on my arrival. Such a course would only serve to alienate him further.'

'Then what do you suggest?'

'Wait until Nicholas is more used to being here, more accustomed to me and the servants around him. He will not miss the woman much then.'

The earl did not answer immediately. He

gazed at her for what seemed to be a long time which Louisa found so disconcerting she was forced to avert her eyes. Finally he put down his empty glass on the tray, saying, 'It shall be as you wish, my dear.' Then, 'I trust you do not find Trevarrick overwhelming at first sight.'

She could not help but chuckle. 'No, I do not.'

'It was foolish of me to venture such a thought. It would be a rare occasion for you to be disconcerted by such a bagatelle.' He shifted slightly before saying, 'I thought it might please you to have some guests here at Christmastide. We have no families living near enough to make casual visits, and you might find it a lonely existence.'

'In Levenham there were several families with whom we exchanged visits, but I can assure you I will not suffer their absence overmuch.'

'But do you object to visitors so soon after our arrival?'

Louisa looked at him again. 'No, but who...?'

'A few friends, not many. I trust that will be no inconvenience to you. If it is the arrangements can be altered.'

She shook her head. 'Indeed not.' Then

she laughed softly. 'In all the excitement of the wedding I quite forgot it will soon be Christmastide.'

There came a knock on the door. A look of irritation crossed the earl's face as he issued the order to enter.

'Mr. Logan is here, my lord,' announced the lackey who entered.

'Show him in.'

Louisa rose to her feet, and the earl turned to her once more. 'I am quite persuaded, Louisa, that all my servants are already captivated by you, and Mr. Logan especially so.'

She blushed slightly and hoped he would think it a reflection of the fire.

'You exaggerate surely, but I believe it always the best policy to have orders carried out by willing hands.'

'From what I have already observed, they will all do your bidding quite gladly.' Lowering his voice slightly he went on, 'Obviously I was right in believing you are the only one who can do anything with my child.'

Louisa turned her face away in embarrassment, murmuring, 'As it is your sole reason for marrying me, it would be dreadful if I failed you in that.'

'You won't.'

Briskly now, she stole a glance at him. 'He was born to be difficult, you know.'

The earl looked alarmed and drew back slightly. 'What...do you mean?'

'It is in his blood, Rohan. His father is an explosive mixture of French and Cornish blood, and his mother Russian. I would say that makes quite a turbulent child.'

The door opened once more and the footman announced the earl's land-steward. Louisa smiled a welcome, glad that so normal a presence would be at their table on this first night, which might have otherwise been fraught with awkwardness.

The earl cast her a long considering look before turning on his heel and welcoming his guest.

Seven

The huge four-poster bed, warmed by a brick, was welcoming after such an eventful day, and Louisa slept heavily. In fact, she had not slept so well since accepting Lord

Rossington's offer of marriage.

She had lain awake for only a short while after retiring to her room, leaving the two men to their port and conversation, for the sound of the sea, incessantly pounding against the rocks, soon lulled her into a dreamless sleep which lasted until Dora came with a cup of chocolate the next morning.

The fire had been mended and roared up the chimney.

'Has his lordship risen yet?' Louisa asked as Dora bustled about the room preparing her mistress's toilette.

She thought about him sleeping at the other side of the door, and the notion made her feel discomforted, for it was so near.

'Yes, ma'am. Went off from here half an hour ago or more.'

Louisa then felt considerable relief. 'He has much to do,' she explained, 'and he is a conscientious employer. Are your quarters comfortable?'

'Yes, ma'am. Being your personal maid, I've been given a room of my own, and a rug for the floor.'

Louisa smiled. 'And so it should be.'

Dora drew back the curtains. 'Oh,

there's no sight of the sea this morning, ma'am. What a shame on your first morning here.'

'Never mind. There will be many other mornings.'

'A mizzling day, it's called.'

Louisa looked at her in surprise and amusement. 'How do you know that, Dora?'

The maid flushed slightly. 'Lucas, one of the footmen, told me, ma'am.'

Louisa continued to eye her in amusement for a moment or two longer before saying, 'Well, I am gratified to see you settling in so well, Dora.' She pulled back the covers. 'There is much to do today, so be pleased to help me dress as quickly as possible.'

Mrs. Pendas made herself available as arranged, and the tour of Trevarrick took some considerable time. Generally, Louisa was pleased with what she saw which was a relief to her as, initially, she did not wish to be engaged for too much of her time with household matters.

The housekeeper performed her duties well, having been appointed by the earl's late mother, and she seemed determined to acquaint the new mistress with every part of the house. Louisa went first to the main salon which contained a good deal of the delicate furniture made popular by the late French queen, Marie Antoinette. She was pleasantly surprised by what she saw as she peered into dusty rooms, unused for almost a decade, where the furniture was shrouded by Holland covers, and concerned herself with the workings of the enormous kitchen and still-room.

'Many of these rooms will be in use at Christmastide,' Louisa informed her. 'We are to have guests, so you should be preparing the rooms now. New curtains are badly needed, but there won't be time to obtain them, so we shall have to contrive as best we can. I will put the matter in hand if you would be so good as to list the requirements. Enlist extra help if you need to do so, Mrs. Pendas.'

The housekeeper smiled. 'Since the passing of the late countess, ma'am, we have been underworked. The chance to put more rooms to use will be welcome.' After a pause she asked, 'Will you be requiring special menus to be prepared, ma'am?'

'I think not, Mrs. Pendas. As long as we have sufficient geese and duck, and plenty of beef and plum pudding, Cook will no doubt prepare them in her usual excellent way.'

Mrs. Pendas smiled. 'I shall tell her, my lady; she will be pleased.' The smile faded abruptly then. 'There is only the nursery for you to inspect now, ma'am.'

She opened the door. Nicholas glanced at them briefly as they entered, a ferocious look on his face. He'd been engrossed in a puzzle whilst Anouska watched him fondly from across the room.

'Good morning, Nicholas, Anouska,' Louisa said brightly.

The nurse bowed slightly, but the child went back to his puzzle. Anouska admonished him, and without looking up the child then said, *'Bonjour, madame.'*

'Oh dear,' Louisa cried to no one in particular. 'I was so certain a boy of Nicholas's age would be able to speak a little English at least.'

At this he looked up indignantly. 'So I can.'

Louisa's eyes opened wide. 'Then why do you not?'

'Because I do not wish to!'

Anouska admonished him yet again, but he appeared unrepentant. Louisa walked further into the nursery which was poorly equipped, possibly unchanged since the earl had occupied it twenty years earlier. Moreover, it was bitterly cold. The hearth was empty as was usual in a nursery, cold being deemed a toughening element for a growing child.

Louisa turned to him, a smile on her face. 'Surely that is rather foolish, Nicholas. After all your Papa and I speak French perfectly well, but none of the servants do, and they will not understand your orders.'

The notion had obviously not occurred to him and he looked astonished. Louisa did not wait for him to recover; casting a further smile at Anouska she added, 'I'll not keep you any longer.'

Mrs. Pendas's lips were drawn tight with disapproval as they left the nursery. 'Such insolence to you, my lady,' she murmured. 'It is too much. Lord Rossington was never like this as a child, rumbustious though he was.'

'His manners will improve, Mrs. Pendas,' Louisa assured her. 'You may be quite certain on that score.'

'I cannot envisage that, if you will pardon me saying so, my lady.'

Once the door had been closed, Louisa said, 'See that the floor is covered with rugs as soon as possible, and I want the fire to be lit at all times.'

The housekeeper obviously did not agree, but merely said, 'It shall be as you wish, my lady,' and went immediately to make the necessary arrangements.

Louisa saw very little of her husband over the next few days which, she suspected, was a deliberate ploy on his part. They shared only dinner together, discussing matters of no real interest. He was busy administering what was a large estate, taking in not only many farms, but several villages too. Louisa was slowly becoming accustomed to life at Trevarrick, and as she had always preferred rusticating to living in Town it suited her well. Of course, it was very different to the life she had previously known. She was after all mistress of a very large establishment, whereas she had only assisted Amy in the running of her more modest one. Most of all Louisa missed her sister's companionship and, of course, that of the children who, by comparison to Nicholas, were little angels. Daily ructions could be heard coming from the nursery suite, when Nicholas had his sport with the maidservants who were foolhardy enough to venture into his domain.

'How do you propose to tackle Nicholas?' the earl asked one evening as they dined, and apparently ran out of conversation on other subjects.

Louisa smiled as she watched him raise his wine-glass to his lips, gazing at her over the rim. 'I have no plan of battle as it were. There is no quick way, I fear, and at the moment I am merely allowing him to grow accustomed to my presence.'

'Once he is used to you we must think about appointing a governess.'

'It is scarce necessary. After all, soon enough he will go away to school. I can do all which is necessary, once he accepts me, naturally.'

'Do you consider that he will?'

She continued to eat her dinner, not the easiest of tasks beneath such critical scrutiny. 'I hope so, otherwise your efforts on his behalf will be all for nothing. I do sometimes wonder what I shall do when Nicholas goes to school and no longer needs my care.'

He put down his glass and frowned. 'I do not quite understand what you mean.'

'I am talking about my position in this household. I am here to care for Nicholas, but once he is at school he will scarce need my ministrations, if we assume he accepts them in the first place.'

His frown seemed to deepen. 'You are my wife, Louisa, for as long as we both live, and you shall receive the entitlements of that position wherever Nicholas happens to be.'

In a high bright voice she answered, 'I'll wager you did not consider that when you made your offer of marriage.'

He smiled crookedly. 'As I recall you were never a good gamester, my dear. Perchance you would lose your wager.'

She drew her gaze away from his, forcing herself to say, 'With regard to his education, in one of my trunks I brought some books which my sister's children found interesting, and also some games.'

'It seems,' he answered, raising his wine-glass once again, 'my task in running this entire estate is the easier one.' A statement which caused Louisa to laugh, albeit uneasily.

When the mizzle lifted she could indeed

see the creek from her window. The yacht no longer rode at anchor though, but Louisa didn't pause to wonder where it might have gone.

The books Dora had unpacked had been sent to the nursery for Nicholas to browse at his own pace with no outside pressure to deter him. She hadn't tried to visit him since that first day and now time enough had elapsed. Louisa decided she must go again. As she walked up the stairs and along the corridor, Louisa was certain that if Anouska was not there her task would be a much easier one. However, she also knew it was far too soon to send the woman away.

A loud rattling noise in the corridor outside the nursery caused her to pause and look around for a cause. A suit of armour, long forgotten, stood in a shadowy corner, and as she looked at it the suit began to clatter even more, swaying from side to side. It was quite alarming to see it move of its own accord.

After a moment or two, however, she recovered from her surprise and approached. Groping behind it she soon located a small arm, and then gently she drew Nicholas out from behind the suit of armour, giving him a wry look.

'For a moment I thought we have ghosts at Trevarrick.'

'It isn't fair!' he protested. 'Mrs. Pendas and two housemaids almost had a seizure when I did that to them.'

'I can well imagine, but it isn't something to be proud of, Nicholas. You might well have caused them real pain, and then you wouldn't have been so proud of yourself.'

He lifted his thin shoulders into a shrug.

'Did you look at the books I sent you?' she asked, holding his arm firmly and guiding him back to the nursery.

'I don't like them.'

'You surprise me. My own nephew enjoyed them when he was your age.'

Anouska was sitting by the fire when they came in, but she immediately got up and shot Louisa a malevolent look which her curtsy didn't quite obscure. Louisa affected to ignore it, merely bidding her a good morning as she glanced about her. She was glad to see that several rugs covered the floor now and that the room had taken on a much more warm and homely look.

'I trust you like the fire,' she ventured.

'I am used to the cold,' he answered.

Undismayed, she continued her inspection of the nursery in greater detail. The books she had sent were piled up on the desk, and she only glanced at them before asking, 'When you were in St. Petersburg did you have lessons?'

'Yes.'

'Yet appear not to have them here, unless I am mistaken.'

'There is no one to give me lessons.' He paused before going on, 'When we came to England, Papa wanted me to have an English governess, but none of them would stay.'

'Why is that?'

He didn't answer, and she ventured, 'Was it because of your bad behaviour, Nicholas?'

'I didn't like any of them. They were English.'

'Naturally,' Louisa answered with a laugh.

'Papa wants me only to be English, but I am Russian.'

'Surely you are both, and as such should you not take advantage of such circumstances?' she replied as his eyes flashed with anger and pride.

'Papa wants me to forget I am Russian.'

114

'I'm persuaded that isn't so, Nicholas, but you are also part English and it is time you learned about that too.'

Idly, Louisa opened one of the books and was shocked to see some of the pages disfigured by several crude drawings.

'Who did this?' she asked.

'I did,' Nicholas answered, showing no sign of repentance. 'I like to draw.'

'Then mayhap I had better supply you with a drawing-block. There is scarce room in a printed book to display your talent.'

Louisa glanced at the drawings again, taking more note of them this time.

'Do you draw anything other than broken dolls, Nicholas?'

He hung his head, and she persisted, 'Is there some reason for it? Something you had back in St. Petersburg?'

When the child looked up his eyes were filled with tears. 'Mama!' he cried, flinging himself into Anouska's waiting arms where he sobbed heartbrokenly until the old woman took him into the adjacent room, murmuring to him all the while.

Although she was naturally disturbed by the child's behaviour, Louisa had little time to brood upon it, for her sleep was disturbed by what she thought was a cry that night.

As she came back to consciousness she first thought it to be the soughing of the wind or the sea breaking against the rocks, but it was an unusually still night and all which could be heard was the ticking of the clock. Moments later she heard it strike three times, and when the chimes began to die away she sank back into the pillows and prepared to sleep again.

But the cry came again, and she could not mistake it this time. With fumbling hands she lit a candle with the tinder-box at the side of the bed. Then, climbing down from the four-poster, she slipped her feet into a pair of slippers. As part of her trousseau Amy had insisted Louisa have fine nightwear, and she slipped her arms into a silk peignoir of great beauty which, ironically, no husband was likely to see.

The corridor was deserted, lit by one or two dying candles which guttered as they burned low. Feeling more than a little foolish and wondering if, perhaps, her head might be too full of the gothic novels she had brought with her, Louisa moved along the corridor very slowly. When she heard the cry again she knew then it was

Nicholas and made haste to the nursery, flinging open the door.

The child was tossing about in his bed in great distress, whilst on an adjacent truckle-bed Anouska lay drunk and insensible, an empty gin-bottle on the floor at her side. Louisa gave her a contemptuous look before rushing to the boy.

She gathered him into her arms, calling his name. 'It is I, Aunt Louisa,' she told him.

He cried out again, and in almost as much distress she said, 'You are safe. Nothing can harm you now.'

'Mama!' he cried. 'Mama.'

She smoothed back his hair from his perspiring face. 'It is I, Aunt Louisa,' she repeated.

At last he opened his eyes and they were filled with horror. Louisa clasped him close to her, and he did not resist her embrace, for it seemed he was still in the grip of the nightmare.

'You're awake now,' she told him in a soothing voice. 'The dream is over.'

His breathing gradually returned to normal and his trembling stilled.

'What alarmed you so?' she asked at last. He looked at her wide-eyed, and, it seemed, uncomprehending. 'It must have been a very bad dream.'

'I dreamed about Mama,' he answered, drawing away from her at last.

'Such a bad dream, though.'

His eyes opened wide with horror at the memory. 'It was Papa. *He* was there too. He killed her. Papa killed her!'

Eight

'Mrs. Pendas, I want you to find a young girl for me,' Louisa said the moment the housekeeper answered her summons the following morning.

'Yes, my lady, but for what duties? We have a full compliment of servants in the house already.'

'I fully appreciate that, but the fact is Anouska is old and needs help with someone as lively as Viscount Danby, I fear, and you may know of a girl who would be suited to the post. I don't want anyone who is already in service here, nor a girl who is too young. Someone from an estate family perhaps.'

Mrs. Pendas's brow furrowed. 'Can't think of anyone off hand, my lady, but I will make enquiries immediately.'

'I'd be obliged if you would. There is an element of urgency in the matter.'

Louisa had been up early that morning, finding sleep difficult to recapture after she'd returned to her bed. The boy's haunted face loomed clearly in her mind even after she had closed her eyes. It meant nothing, she told herself. It was only a nightmare. Children often had bad dreams.

She found him busily drawing on the block she had provided, and it came as a relief to her to see him looking so normal. He must have forgotten all about it by now, she thought.

Anouska looked ill, as well she might, and averted her face. Louisa ignored her and was glad to see Nicholas drawing ordinary objects like boats and crude horses.

'Those are very good,' she told him. After a moment she went to the window. 'It's a fine morning. I'm going to walk down to the creek. Would you like to come with me?'

Immediately she could see that he was

torn between the wish to go and the now habitual desire to be disobedient.

'You can show me the way,' she added. 'I'm still a stranger here. You must know your way around the estate by now.'

'Oh very well,' the boy conceded, and Louisa asked Anouska to bring his coat and gloves, and outdoor boots, something she did reluctantly.

The air was bracing, and they walked briskly down the path and away from the house. Neither of them mentioned the previous night's events, for she was certain it would remain far longer in her memory than in his.

'One day you will own all this,' she told him after they had walked in silence for a while. 'Does the prospect please you?'

'I have estates in Russia too.'

'When you're a man you will have to spend part of your time in St. Petersburg and part here.'

'When I am old enough,' he said darkly, 'I will leave this place for good.'

'That would be a shame, indeed. After all, your Papa takes great pride in Trevarrick, which is a fine estate, and so did your Grandpapa.'

He didn't answer, but when he did

Louisa was startled by the question. 'All my cousins in St. Petersburg had brothers and sisters. Shall I have brothers and sisters too now my father has a new wife?'

Louisa hardly knew what to say in answer. She hadn't given much thought to the fact their marriage would lack children. She supposed it would be assumed that such an occurrence was mere misfortune. The earl already had his heir, so their childless state would hardly be a loss to him.

'That,' she answered presently, 'is something I cannot say.' Then in a deliberate ploy to change the subject, 'Tell me about your life in St. Petersburg. It must have been quite different to how we live at Trevarrick.'

His eyes glowed with genuine pleasure at the memory. 'It was wonderful there. The house was always full of people. Mama liked to hold parties, and everyone who came looked so splendid; the officers from the Queen's guard in their uniforms and the ladies wearing jewels which sparkled in the candle light. From my bedroom window in our palace I could see boats from all over the world sailing into the harbour.'

'You like boats, it seems,' Louisa commented as they reached the creek, trying not to let the images of the earl's life in St. Petersburg or his lovely princess dampen her spirits further.

'I'd like to be a sailor when I grow up, and sail the seven seas.'

'Mayhap your Papa will allow you to be commissioned into the navy when you are grown, if you are still of the same mind.'

At the mention of his father he glowered and stubbed his booted foot against a rock. 'I want to fight Pirates not Frenchies.'

Louisa laughed softly. 'I confess I cannot understand why anyone would wish to sail any boat, Nicholas.'

'You did not like the yacht?'

'In all truth I did not.'

'I am a very good sailor,' he boasted. 'Captain Knott told me so.'

'I don't doubt it. You must have inherited that ability from your father's family.'

When he looked at her curiously she asked, 'Do you not know about Sir Patrick Keenan, your ancestor?'

He shook his head and she went on, 'He was a privateer in the service of Queen Elizabeth, who eventually conferred upon

122

him the earldom of Rossington.'

She watched for his reaction and she was certain he was impressed. However, moments later he said, 'My uncle, Prince Rascoff, is a general in Queen Catherine's army.'

'But it is to the sea you feel drawn,' she pointed out.

He didn't reply to that, and she asked, 'Where do you suppose the yacht has gone now?'

He looked up at her, his brow furrowed. 'Do you not know?'

'I haven't asked and no one has told me.'

'To London, of course, to bring Papa's guests.'

'Of course!' Louisa cried. 'I quite forgot. We are to have guests. I wonder who they are, Nicholas.'

'Do you not know?' he asked in amazement.

'No! Do you?'

He shook his head, and she said, 'It will be a surprise for us both. Come, let us return to the house. The wind is freshening again and I wouldn't like you to become chilled.'

'I am used to the cold,' he boasted. 'In

St. Petersburg it was much colder than here. In the winter the Neva freezes over and no ships can sail into port.'

Louisa gave an expressive shudder. 'I would hate that, Nicholas. I like the sun on my face.'

'Mama always said that ruins a lady's complexion.'

She looked at him fondly. 'I dare say she was correct, but in the summer we can spend much more time outdoors, playing games on the lawn.'

'I don't like games,' he answered, reverting to his former hostility.

They began to walk back. 'There is one called croquet, and another I know you'll particularly like called shuttlecock. My nephew is very good at it.'

'I don't care.'

'Well,' Louisa mused, 'he is two years older than you, so perchance you would not do as well as he.'

The resulting response was just as she expected. 'I shall play even better than he. I shall show you how good I am!'

'We shall see at the first possible moment,' she told him, a little breathlessly as they began to climb the path, which had not seemed to slope downwards nearly as steeply as it went up.

'I'll wager I can reach the house before you!'

He rushed ahead of her despite her cries. Louisa began to run after him but could not hope to catch up. By the time the path levelled out again he was nowhere to be seen, and when she reached the house, feeling rather out of breath, the earl came cantering round the corner, astride his black mare.

'How fortunate we should arrive back together,' he said, sliding to the ground and handing the reins to his groom.

Louisa had not seen him since Nicholas had his nightmare, and in view of the boy's outburst felt somewhat discomposed.

He regarded her for a moment or two before saying, 'The Cornish air appears to agree with you, my dear. Your cheeks are ruddy and your eyes bright.'

'Mayhap I should make a habit of a good brisk walk every day.'

'An excellent idea,' he agreed as they walked into the hall.

He sat down, and as the footman started to pull off his muddy hessians and Louisa allowed another servant to remove her fur-lined cloak, he added, 'Logan was enquiring after your health again today.'

She was gazing into one of the mirrors, tucking in fine wisps of hair which had come free of their pins. 'How kind of him,' she responded, somewhat automatically.

The earl, now wearing clean boots, got to his feet. 'I do believe you have made a conquest there, Louisa.'

What she detected as mockery on his part angered her and she turned round to face him again. The half-smile on his face confirmed her suspicions, and it moved her to retort, 'It is not unknown.'

The smile faded, and as she began to walk up the stairs he fell into step with her. 'What is this I hear about Nicholas spending the night in your dressing-room?'

'It was only for part of the night. He had a nightmare, you see, and was terrified of being left alone.'

'Where was Anouska whilst all this was ensuing?'

At the landing he took out his pocket-watch and glanced at it before putting it away.

Louisa drew a sigh. 'She was drunk.'

Anger flared in his eyes and the colour which crept into his face seemed to highlight the hollows in his cheeks.

'I see,' he said, letting out a long breath. 'I should not be surprised. In Russia there is a drink brewed by peasants called vodka, and I always suspected she was addicted to it although it is difficult to detect. Gin is altogether much easier. Well, 'tis plain she must be removed whether you are in agreement or not.'

'I am. We cannot tolerate such dereliction of duty. In fact, I have instructed Mrs. Pendas to find a reliable girl to take her place.'

He nodded his agreement. 'It disturbs me to hear about Nicholas. He used to be plagued by nightmares, but I believed them to be a rarity now.'

'That might be so. It was the first I have witnessed, but all the same he was dreadfully distraught. I could not leave him alone in all conscience.'

Stiffly he answered, 'I did not ask you to.'

He began to walk away, and she said then, 'You are angry with me.'

'Only when you misjudge me,' he answered, still with his back to her.

'You misunderstand *me*, Rohan.'

He glanced at her, smiling faintly. 'Let us call it a draw.'

Before he could walk away she asked, a little breathlessly, 'Is it possible for us to ride out with you one morning?' When he turned to look at her again, she added, 'I believe it would be beneficial.'

'I'll not gainsay anything you suggest in that respect, Louisa. You have improved his demeanour in this short time.'

Her eyes widened. 'I scarce think so.'

'But it is true. There have been few to-dos of late, no servant girl has had the vapours, no crashing of mysterious articles to startle us out of our wits. Indeed you have improved his manners.'

'I have merely begun to divert his energies,' she told him.

His eyebrows rose a fraction. 'Pray continue by all means.'

He was about to go again when he remembered something, tossing a letter in her direction.

'This arrived for you earlier. From Mrs. Mulcaster no doubt.'

Louisa bore it to her own sitting-room and settled down to the pleasure of reading it. The sight of Amy's careful hand brought waves of nostalgia washing over her and a tear to her eye, but that did not mar her joy at hearing all the on-dits from Town and,

128

more importantly, news of the children.

'I trust you are now accustomed to being addressed as Lady Rossington,' Amy wrote. 'For myself I never tire of speaking of my sister, the Countess of Rossington.'

Louisa smiled to herself, for it seemed Amy had quite forgotten her prejudice against the earl. She read on eagerly. 'A Count Lanchovsky has been in London of late and he knows Rossington well. He was also acquainted with the late Princess Rascoff whom Rossington married. Beautiful but wilful, Lanchovsky describes her, but I was most disturbed at his mention of some wicked rumours circulating in St. Petersburg after she had died. No doubt Rossington has told you the entire tale, and I was so angry to hear such wicked lies repeated. I felt bound to tell the Count so.'

Louisa read the last part of the letter several times and was indeed still doing so when a knock at the door made her start. Quickly she folded the letter before giving the summons to enter.

Although shaken by what she had read she presented an air of calm as the housekeeper came into the room.

'I'm sorry to disturb you, my lady, but

I thought you'd like to know I've found a girl you might consider.'

Louisa was immediately diverted. 'Well done, Mrs. Pendas. When may I speak to her?'

The housekeeper flushed with pleasure at such praise. 'She waits your pleasure below now, my lady.'

Louisa immediately put the letter into her pocket. 'Show her up with no further delay.' As the woman hastened to do her bidding she added, 'Oh, do please tell me a little about her first.'

'Well, my lady, she's of the fisherfolk in Kilrannan. Respectable people, so I'm told. She's fifteen years old and never been in service before.'

'She would seem to be the right kind, Mrs. Pendas. You may send her to me.'

The girl was as thin as a board, shivering, perhaps with fear or because she wore thread-bare clothing and the three-mile walk from Kilrannan would have chilled her through.

'Come in and sit down,' Louisa invited after the girl had curtsied.

She came into the room, gazing about her in awe, and Louisa indicated a chair near to the fire. The girl perched nervously on the edge of the seat, appearing ill at ease. No doubt it was the first time in her life she had been in any house other than her own modest cottage which would be in its entirety much smaller than this drawing-room.

'Mrs. Pendas omitted to tell me your name,' Louisa ventured as she too sat down.

'Jenny, my lady,' she answered as she folded her hands together on her lap. 'Jenny Quint.'

'Did Mrs. Pendas tell you what the nature of your duties would be here?' The girl nodded, and Louisa went on, 'Lord Danby has lately come from St. Petersburg and naturally the move has unsettled him somewhat.'

'Yes, ma'am, I understand.'

Louisa somehow doubted that she did, but asked, 'Why have you not gone into service before now?'

'Me Ma died five years gone and Pa's on the boats. There was only me to look after the children.'

'Your brothers and sisters?' The girl nodded, and Louisa asked, 'How many?'

'Eight left, my lady, so's I know how to look after a little one.'

Louisa smiled wryly. 'This one might be more trouble than your eight, Jenny.'

'I don't mind, my lady. This chance to work at the big house is too good to miss. You'll not be sorry if you take me on, my lady. Never!'

'Lord Danby already has a nursemaid who came to England with him. You might find her odd at first, but don't mind that. Don't try to take her place, but just allow the boy to get to know you in his own time and I'm sure all will be well. Whatever he does, and I admit he can be difficult, treat him kindly and he will become attached to you in time.'

The girl beamed. 'Yes, my lady,' and then, 'Does that mean I'm to be taken on?'

'I think you can be given a chance.'

The girl beamed again. 'I'm ever so grateful, my lady, really I am.'

'Oh, please don't be. Your work will not be easy. When can you come?'

'Now, my lady.'

Louisa got to her feet and, crossing the room, she rang for a servant. The girl looked at her expectantly as she said, 'I'll ask Mrs. Pendas to find you some suitable clothing.'

'Thank you, ma'am.'

As soon as she had gone, Louisa's satisfaction faded, and almost unwillingly she brought out Amy's letter and began to read it once again.

Nine

There must have been some truth in Jenny's claim that she could handle children, for her absorption into the household was less stormy than Louisa expected. Anouska, she suspected, found him too much for her to handle alone and was a little relieved to have more time to sup her gin. Nicholas protested, of course, but Louisa countered this with the offer of a bedchamber of his own, which immediately appealed, and she arranged for him to be put in a room not far from her own. There was a dressing-room attached where Jenny could sleep, but he would have a room entirely his own away from the nursery for the first time. It was far too tempting an offer to lose by a display of temper, and so Jenny was accepted grudgingly.

At Louisa's suggestion the earl put in motion plans for Anouska to return to St. Petersburg in the most diplomatic way he could contrive.

'I survived the intricacies and machinations of the St. Petersburg court, which is no mean feat, but matters pertaining my own son tend to defeat me,' he said darkly, which made Louisa laugh.

Then, one morning as Christmastide approached, unexpectedly he joined her for breakfast. At first she was startled, for she rarely saw him before dinner, but then, almost unwillingly, she experienced a feeling of pleasure. Apart from his detached interest in her there was very little pretence of married life. He had promised none, but nevertheless her solitude was sometimes melancholy.

'This is a rare honour,' she ventured as he sat down.

'I am gratified you deem it so,' he answered with a smile which revealed very little. 'I have arranged for Anouska to leave today,' he announced whilst she was still looking at him curiously. 'Now that he has grown more accustomed to you and the new servant you engaged the time has come.'

'Indeed,' she answered, feeling none the less apprehensive. 'He will survive her loss and recover. It is wrong for him to become too attached to anyone, much less a servant.'

'She and I never saw eye to eye even in St. Petersburg, so her influence has not been a good one, but she has been well rewarded for her devotion, and I believe she will be happier with my... with Natalia's family where she belongs.' As Louisa stared at him he looked at her at last. 'Do you still wish to ride out with me?'

'Indeed I do,' she answered with greater enthusiasm than she intended.

'Then today would be a good time. It will save Anouska weeping over the boy all morning.'

Louisa threw down her napkin. 'If you'll excuse me I'll have Jenny put him into some riding-clothes.'

As she made to pass him he caught her hand and drew her back. She looked down at him questioningly, unable to read the expression in his dark, brooding eyes which he had bestowed with such devastating effect upon his son.

It seemed he was about to say something, but then he let her go, returning to his breakfast without a word whilst Louisa hurried from the room, her heart beating unaccountably fast.

It was mandatory for Nicholas to refuse to comply with any request made of him and, after changing into a jade green riding-habit herself, she found him resisting all the girl's attempts to get him to wear his riding-clothes.

'Why are you being so obstinate?' Louisa asked bluntly as she drew on her gloves.

'I don't wish to go out just now.'

'Is it because you cannot ride?'

The boy bridled. 'Of course I can! I ride as well as my father.'

'I cannot believe that.'

'You'll see!' he cried, rushing to dress in the clothes he had hitherto scorned.

Louisa smiled to herself and went to wait in the hall downstairs where the earl joined her shortly afterwards.

'The horses are being brought round,' he told her in the now customary detached manner he employed towards her.

Louisa did not take it amiss as he had rarely expressed warmth to anyone in her presence, but only now did it occur to her as odd.

'Does Nicholas deem to join us?'

'He will be here.'

He gave her a laconic look. 'How did you manage to persuade him? What bribe did you offer?'

She looked him directly in the eye. 'None. I merely cast doubt on his riding ability, and true to the Rossington pride he will be here to prove me wrong.'

He gave her a long, disbelieving look before saying, 'That is quite remarkable. I had made up my mind you would be obliged to drag him forcibly down the stairs.'

'That is not the way to get things done, Rohan.'

'Evidently. I have given you a free hand to deal with him as you see fit, Louisa, and you are doing exceedingly well, I own, but I am not at all certain it is right for him to sleep so close to our own apartments. It is not customary.'

'I thought it necessary. He is not like an ordinary child, which you must own. It could not be done, of course, if there were other children to consider.'

He stared at her hard, and her voice died

in her throat. She was obliged to look away from such a disconcerting stare.

Moments later Nicholas came clattering down the stairs and, dressed for riding, he looked like a miniature version of his father.

The grooms arrived at almost the same time with the horses, two thoroughbreds and a pony for Nicholas.

'When shall I have a horse of my own?' the child asked, looking askance at the pony.

'When you are able to ride one,' his father replied.

Whilst the earl lifted his son into the saddle, Louisa allowed one of the grooms to hand her up. When the earl swung himself into the saddle they set off, Nicholas saying, 'I can ride like a cossack!'

'What is a cossack?' Louisa enquired.

'They're a fierce race of horsemen from Russia,' the earl replied. 'They tend to rebel against the Queen from time to time and have to be put down.'

'They eat people,' Nicholas added.

'How horrid,' Louisa complained, shuddering, which delighted the boy.

When she glanced at her husband she

was surprised to see that he was smiling too, an all too rare occurrence.

'Do you enjoy riding?' he asked a moment later.

'Very much. At Levenham I rode as often as I could. It's good riding country.'

'It can be rough around here, but you should try to get out more. Take Nicholas with you; he needs the practice.'

'I do not!'

The earl silenced him with a fierce look, and Louisa said gently, 'I shall go out once I have less to occupy me in the house.'

They passed several farms where the workers paused to pull at their forelocks. Mark Logan joined them at their first stop, the home farm on the edge of the Trevarrick grounds. The farmer's wife was all but overcome at having both the master and mistress call, as she explained that butter and cheese were delivered every week and milk collected daily. Afterwards they were given ale and freshly baked cakes whilst Nicholas chased the geese outside in the yard.

'Your presence will delight all the tenants,' Mark Logan told her at the first opportunity.

'I must confess my purpose was for Lord Danby to see something of his eventual responsibilities, nothing more.'

The young man frowned. 'He is a little young for that surely. It will be many years, God willing, before he inherits.'

'It will do him no harm to develop a sense of responsibility, and the fresh air is bound to be beneficial.'

'You have certainly improved his manners since your arrival if you will forgive my presumption in saying so, my lady.'

Louisa gave him a grin. 'You are only saying what everyone else knows, Mr. Logan. It seems everyone at Trevarrick are seasoned soldiers in the struggle against Nicholas.'

He roared with laughter before saying, 'If that is so, my lady, you bear your battle scars well.'

Out of the corner of her eye Louisa noticed that the earl was frowning at them, and she wondered if he regarded it undignified for her to be making a jest with his land-steward, and some of her pleasure died.

A short time later they all left to visit other farms and one of the villages. Nicholas appeared to be quite happy, which relieved Louisa, although she dreaded his reaction when he discovered his nurse gone. That thought was never far from her mind.

Their last stop was at the cottage of Will Harden, who cared for the earl's beagles and retrievers, a stop which delighted Nicholas, and Louisa was pleasantly surprised that the earl should have thought of it. There were several litters of puppies, and the boy enjoyed himself as much as he had chasing the geese.

'Harden is the best trainer in Cornwall,' the earl told her as they watched Nicholas trying to catch one of the puppies. 'I'm fortunate to have him in my service.'

'From all I have seen you are a benevolent master,' she replied, knowing it to be the truth.

He smiled faintly. 'If my French relatives had taken heed of our ways, the King would still be alive and so would they.'

'You'll find that there are a number of good retrievers for your sport this time,' Mr. Logan explained.

'I'm looking forward to some shooting when my guests arrive,' the earl replied.

Louisa moved away as they continued to discuss the finer points of the gun dogs, and whilst she watched Nicholas enjoying himself a notion suddenly came into her head. Quickly she walked back to the two men.

As she did so she was aware that they both watched her. Mark Logan was blatantly admiring, and the knowledge caused her some small pleasure, but it was difficult as always even to hazard a guess at what the earl was thinking. His expression betrayed nothing but she felt he noted everything.

'Is it possible for Nicholas to have one of the puppies for his own?' The earl displayed surprise at her request, and she went on eagerly, 'I am sure it would help divert his mind.'

'From what?'

'From mischief amongst other things,' she answered with a laugh.

Mark Logan gave her an encouraging smile as the earl said, 'More like he will tie the poor beast in knots.'

'Oh, you truly wrong him,' Louisa protested and was relieved when his face relaxed.

'Very well, if you truly believe it a benefit to him I will ask Harden to make a choice.'

142

As he strode away Louisa smiled after him, but when Mr. Logan spoke she gave him her attention.

'I am persuaded you know he can refuse you nothing.'

It was a statement which caused her to look away again in confusion, longing to tell him that not all men looked upon her with admiration.

Only a few minutes later the earl returned to tell her, 'Nicholas has made his own choice after all.'

Louisa could see then that the boy was struggling to hold a squirming puppy, and she laughed. 'It takes so little to make a child happy.'

Her husband gave her a dark look. 'Would that it were so easy for everyone else. I believe we should start back now. It will be dark within the hour. Will you call Nicholas?'

Obediently she did so, and the boy came running up to her, his cheeks flushed from a combination of fresh air and pleasure.

'Have you seen my new dog, Aunt Louisa? He looks very fine. He's going to be all mine, for ever!'

'You're very fortunate, you know, and you must look after him carefully.'

143

'Oh, I will. I shall guard him with my life.'

Louisa laughed. 'That is for him to do for you. Have you decided on a name?'

'Mr. Harden says he is already named Rollo.'

'Well, that is a good name, don't you agree, Mr. Logan?'

'Indeed I do.'

Nicholas looked even more pleased until his father called him and the light of pleasure faded from his eyes. When he hesitated to go Louisa urged him quietly, and he went at last.

Mark Logan handed Louisa into the saddle, saying in a low voice, 'Is it possible you will accompany his lordship again in the near future?'

'I think not,' she answered, smiling down at him. 'I am occupied at the house and will be even more so when our guests arrive.'

'That will be a loss to the entire estate.'

The earl began to ride away with Nicholas in pursuit. Louisa dug in her own heels, saying, 'Good bye, Mr. Logan.'

When she glanced back moments later he was still standing where she had left him, gazing after her.

They rode back to Trevarrick in silence. Louisa wasn't certain whether the earl was being normally quiet or perhaps displaying disapproval of her friendship with his land-steward.

It came as a relief as they reached the headland when Nicholas pointed out to sea.

'Only look, Aunt Louisa! The yacht. It's out in the channel.'

Sure enough the *Natalia* was in full sail and heading for Trevarrick creek.

'Our guests are about to arrive,' the earl told her, breaking his silence at last.

'This is quite a surprise,' she answered, somewhat coldly.

'To me too; I was not certain when they would arrive.'

Louisa was sceptical of that excuse, but made no reply.

'I trust that all is in readiness, Louisa,' he said moments later.

His cold tone irritated, although it was in no way more than usual.

'Everything has been in readiness for days. Even if I were incapable of it, your servants are not.'

She turned her horse, digging her heels into its flanks and rode quickly back towards the house. The horses' hooves pounded the gorse on the headland, and the wind from the sea bit into her face. She could hear him behind her and it gave her a deal of satisfaction to know he could not catch up with her until she reached the house.

Before she could dismount, though, he had caught the reins in his hands. As she raised her furious gaze to his she was amazed to see he was actually amused by her anger.

'My God, Louisa, this is the first time I have seen you in anything resembling a pucker. I am bound to say it becomes you well.'

With her anger kindled again she allowed the groom to help her dismount. The earl was still looking amused as he handed his reins to the groom, and it was then that Nicholas caught up with them.

'I must show Rollo to Anouska!' he cried.

Louisa started after him. 'Oh no! Nicholas! Nicholas!'

But the child was already charging up the stairs, the puppy in his arms. Louisa would have followed, only the earl caught her arm, saying, 'Leave him alone. He has to know. Let us hope that the puppy is sufficient to divert him.'

Louisa doubted if it would be, and as she pulled off her riding-hat she felt sick at heart. Just when their visitors were arriving was no time for Nicholas to revert to being an *enfant terrible*.

'How long has she been gone?'

'Long enough to be far away,' he replied. 'I have given my servants instructions to make sure she is put on a ship which goes to St. Petersburg.' Then he added, 'We had best prepare ourselves for a turbulent scene.'

The earl had only just been divested of his boots when all too soon Nicholas came rushing back down the stairs, the distress evident on his face.

'She's gone. Anouska's gone! Jenny says she's gone for good.'

Louisa rushed forward in a vain attempt to avert a scene in front of the earl, whose face was already looking as black as thunder.

'Nicholas, let me explain...'

'No!' He drew back, and somewhere on the landing she was aware of Jenny hovering, pale-faced and unable to decide what to do.

147

The child stared at his father with pure hatred. 'It was you who sent her away. I know it was you!'

'Nicholas,' the earl ordered in a voice that would have shattered ice. 'Be silent.'

But the boy was too far gone in his grief to stop now. 'You did send her away, and I know why. Because she knows what you've done!'

From being purple with fury, the earl's face suddenly drained of all colour. His hands were clenched into fists at his side.

Louisa looked to him fearfully, but once again the child claimed her attention as he turned on his heels and ran, sobbing hysterically, upstairs again.

After hesitating a moment or two, Louisa shot her husband another fearful look and then hurried up the stairs after her stepson.

Ten

Louisa smoothed the thick, dark hair from his brow as Nicholas lay in the bed, pale but calm now.

Jenny came fearfully into the room

148

almost on tip toe, and immediately Louisa said, 'Ask Cook to prepare a posset, Jenny, if you please.'

Nodding, the girl withdrew again, and Louisa told him, 'Nicholas, you and I must have a talk.' He didn't reply, and she went on regardless, 'You must think about this from Anouska's point of view as well as your own. She is old and often ill too, and this is a land which is very strange to her. She isn't even part English, as you are. She has no friends or relatives here. She will be much happier with your mother's family in St. Petersburg. And only think how miserable she would be once you are away at school.'

There was still no response and she went on, 'You saw a little today of what will, in time to come, belong to you. It isn't just a right, Nicholas; it's a responsibility too. The tenants look to us for an example and you must give it to them, not indulge in tantrums when something does not quite please you.'

'She said she would never leave me.'

'That was before you had us, Nicholas. Now you have me and Jenny to look out for you.'

He looked at her at last. 'Don't *you* ever

leave me, *matouchka*.'

'I won't. I promise, but you must also give me your word you will beg your Papa's pardon.'

The hard look came onto his face again before he answered, 'Oh very well, if it pleases you.'

'You must also please your father. Now try to sleep a while, and when you wake up I will bring you some supper.' She glanced out of the window to where the yacht had anchored in the creek. 'I must go and greet our guests, but I will come back to see you later.'

She waited a little longer until it seemed he was asleep before leaving the room, by which time a procession was making its way from the creek.

Deep in thought over Nicholas's outburst it therefore came as a shock for Louisa to come face to face with her husband.

'Is he calmer now?' he asked, genuinely anxious.

'Yes, he is asleep. And he will apologise to you for the outburst.'

'That is unimportant,' he answered, much to her surprise, and she realised he was still shaken from the boy's words.

More surprising, she realised then that

150

he was ill at ease with her. After a moment he said in a muted tone, 'I must go downstairs to await our guests. Join me when you are able.'

As he walked away she hurried after him. 'What does *matouchka* mean? Do you know?'

His eyes narrowed as he looked at her. 'Where did you hear that?'

'From Nicholas. I think he called me it. It isn't rude, is it?'

He smiled faintly. 'Congratulations, my dear. It literally means 'little mother'.'

Louisa had no time to experience pleasure at that revelation, for she made haste to her own room at last. She took as little time as possible to wash and change out of her riding-habit, taking care, however, to wear a gown which was both fashionable and flattering.

When she went downstairs again the earl's friends were arriving. His mood, she was glad to see, had become quite affable in a way she rarely witnessed, and it was the first time she was forced to admit that her husband had a side to his character she did not know about.

Being greeted in the hall was a man whose extravagance of dress did not proclaim him a devotee of Beau Brummell.

'Allow me to present my wife,' the earl said as she came down the stairs. 'Louisa, this is an old friend of mine, Sir Max Verrender.'

She greeted him warmly, although she did not much like the way the man eyed her, far too boldly for a true gentleman.

As he took her hand and raised it to his lips he said, never taking his eyes from hers, 'My lady, I always admired Rossington his good taste, but never more than now.'

To her annoyance she could feel the colour rush to her cheeks and was glad of the arrival of another visitor, an affected young man by the name of Dudley Hopewell, who, at least, did not regard her in the least lasciviously.

'The divine Sophie has not set foot on deck since leaving London,' he announced, 'and would you believe, Rossington, I have been unable to partake of a drop of port. Simply couldn't even look at the bottle.'

'This gentleman is the son of a naval officer, would you believe, Louisa?' the earl explained as she eyed the newcomer with amusement.

'Ah, but pressed into service. It was seven full years before he set eyes on his homeland again.'

'Don't believe any of the Banbury Tales he is certain to tell you.'

'Now I am forewarned, I shall not,' she answered, 'But you shall serve to amuse me, Mr. Hopewell.'

'It will be my greatest honour, my lady. Rossington has kept you hidden from mortals less fortunate than he for far too long a time.'

'But you may only amuse her ladyship when I permit,' Sir Max warned him. 'I have made up my mind to get to know Lady Rossington whilst I am here, and I will brook no interference in my scheme.'

Louisa reflected that it would be pleasant to have such lively company for a few weeks. Only then did she realise how insulated from the outside world she had become.

'My wife has other matters to occupy her,' the earl warned in a semi-jocular manner.

'Really, Rossington,' the other man teased, 'I had not thought you to possess such a jealous nature.'

The earl looked vexed at the other man's interpretation of his words, but then another arrival was announced.

'Rossington! My dear. How I have missed you!'

Louisa swung round on her heel at the sound of the heavily accented voice in time to see a woman sweeping into the hall. She was dressed in the height of fashion, accompanied by a negro page, and immediately claiming everyone's attention as if it were the most natural thing in the world.

'It seems we have been travelling for ever. *Mon dieu*. How glad I am to be here.'

The earl raised her hand to his lips. '*Ma chére* Sophie, you look more wonderful every time I clap eyes upon you.'

Suddenly Louisa realised she had seen this woman before—in the earl's high perch phaeton as it travelled along Oxford Street. Then as now she was a woman to be admired, with eyes like emeralds and hair the colour of gingerbread. Her green gown trimmed with gold braid and the matching pelisse did nothing to detract from her beauty.

As the greetings were made Louisa

watched as unfamiliar emotions welled up inside her.

When suddenly she caught the eye of Sir Max she noticed he was looking at her with a mixture of malice and amusement, as if he were well aware of her resentment. Perhaps all women resented this rare beauty.

The newcomer caught sight of Louisa then and drew away from the earl at last. 'And this must be your bride.'

'Louisa, meet my cousin, Madame Sophie Duvalle.'

Louisa shot him a questioning look as the woman clasped her hands and kissed her lightly on both cheeks. 'I see my charming but neglectful cousin has failed to tell you we are related.'

'I am afraid so,' she answered shakily.

'He is so very remiss. However, we shall get to know each other. *Bien.*' She kept hold of Louisa's hands as she turned to the earl, 'Your bride is charming, Rossington. *Trés belle.*'

The earl smiled ironically. 'I am so relieved you approve Sophie.'

She laughed delightedly at his irony, and he went on, 'No doubt you will wish to refresh yourselves before dinner. The servants will show you to your rooms.'

Louisa didn't know what to say, especially when Madame Duvalle blew a kiss from the stairs towards them. She was saved the trouble in any event, for the earl immediately said, 'You'll be pleased to learn that the bolts of cloth you ordered have arrived too.'

She found she had to force a smile to her face. 'Splendid. If you'll excuse me, Rohan, I shall go now and make certain they are all in order.'

Having guests in the house certainly changed everything. Even though Louisa could not quite persuade herself to like her husband's guests, their presence did at least ensure she saw more of him. Previous to their arrival they met over dinner, and afterwards she was invariably left to retire to her own drawing-room to sew or to read until bedtime.

Now he was in the house at most times, although it was true it was spent playing billiards with his friends, riding out on the estate, or shooting duck. Madame Duvalle invariably accompanied them, and no one deemed it odd that Louisa did not.

However, although her first concern

was Nicholas, once he was in bed the evenings, she had to admit, were more lively. When the men joined the ladies in the large drawing-room, Louisa was usually prevailed upon to play the harpsichord, which she did well. Sir Max Verrender invariably insisted on turning her music whilst the earl and his cousin often shared a sofa, talking in low whispers of which she was always aware.

Nor did Madame Duvalle retire early. Her capacity for drink was almost as great as that of the gentlemen, and Louisa often heard them retiring noisily to their chambers long after she, herself, had been forced to go up.

Louisa could not dislike Sophie Duvalle, for she was gay and good-natured, but neither could she take her to her heart. For one thing it was difficult for her to credit the outgoing French-woman a relative of the haughty Rossingtons, and try as she would she could not prevent herself resenting the time her husband spent in the woman's company, illogical as that must be. Sir Max's unmistakable admiration for her, although unsought on her part, was in a small way a balm. However, several times she was obliged to avoid being alone with him, for on those occasions his admiration was in danger of becoming too ardent. Despite the earl's disinterest in her charms, Louisa was not prepared to allow Sir Max much head in this matter.

'We have had so little time to talk to each other,' the French-woman complained one evening when they adjourned to the drawing-room, leaving the men to their port.

As Louisa took up her sewing she reflected sourly that if Madame Duvalle did not spend so much time with the earl, she would have an opportunity to converse with everyone. Needless to say, the thought remained an unspoken one.

'You may be aware I devote a good deal of my time to Lord Danby who still feels the loss of his mother sorely, and the break from the only homeland he has known has been a wrench for one so young.'

Madame Duvalle sighed. 'Indeed, he has been most unfortunate in his young life, but I can see that his fortunes have been reversed most happily now. You have lifted a great burden from your husband's shoulders.'

Only too well aware of it, Louisa was

annoyed that Sophie Duvalle should know too.

'Did you know Rossington's first wife?' she asked in a careful tone a moment later, concentrating hard at the same time on her needlework.

'*Mais non.* I never visited St. Petersburg and she did not come to England—or France—but I know about her.' She laughed lightly. 'I do not think we should have been friends, she and I. Poor Rossington did not have such an easy life as her husband, I am certain. It is obvious why he has been so concerned for the child, and from all I have observed with good cause.'

'His manners are now much improved, as you have no doubt noted, Madame.'

Sophie Duvalle threw up her hands in a typically Gallic gesture. 'His manners, yes, and due entirely to you, I am persuaded. His mind is what I mean. *Comprendez?*'

Louisa put down her sewing at last. 'No, madame, I regret I do not.'

'*L'insanité, naturellement.*'

Louisa's eyes narrowed in disbelief. 'Madame, I would be the first to admit his behaviour goes beyond the pale at times, but Nicholas is as sane as you or I.'

'Now, perhaps, I agree, but Rossington is concerned about later. After his Grand-mama and mother...'

Annoyed Louisa retorted, 'I really don't know what you may mean, *madame.*'

Once again the woman threw up her hands. *'Mon dieu! L'imbecile.* It is plain to me that Rossington has been remiss with you, my dear Louisa.'

She was not at all pleased at being addressed with such familiarity by this woman, but that was of no importance now.

'The child's grandmother,' Sophie Duvalle went on to explain, 'died insane. Her attic, as they say, was to let, and poor Natalia went the same way. *Enfin,* you now understand the better poor Rossington's concern for his offspring, and well placed it is to my mind.'

Louisa did indeed understand it now and she was deeply shocked by Madame Duvalle's revelation. Angry too, that the earl had not told her of it himself. But she reflected, at last, there were a good many things he had not told her and with good reason.

'Do not let the knowledge alarm you, *ma chére.* There is nought you can do, and

I am certain you understand Rossington's reluctance to discuss it with you.'

But he discussed it with you, she wanted to cry out in frustration and anger.

Instead she picked up her sewing again. 'We have scarce had time, *madame.* There has been so much to occupy us both since we came to Trevarrick.'

'So I observed. Rossington is fortunate to have taken a wife who is so concerned with household matters. You have made great improvements, I own.'

Louisa looked at her again with surprise. 'So you have visited Trevarrick before.'

The woman laughed lightly. *'Mais oui.* It is like home to me.'

Such an admission only served to irritate Louisa again, but once more she didn't show it. 'Is...there anything else I should know relating to my husband or stepson?' she couldn't help but ask.

'I think not. What I have told you is enough, *hein?'*

Louisa managed to smile. 'Indeed. Rossington is notoriously remiss, as you have pointed out. He mentioned not a word about you,' she said sweetly. 'Are you very closely related?'

'Not really. On his Mama's side of

161

course, but however distantly we are related Rossington never forgets his obligations, for when I was forced to flee *ma belle* France it was he who offered me the use of his Bloomsbury house for as long as I needed a home. That was kind of him, was it not?'

Kind, indeed, Louisa reflected angrily. She felt as if someone were slowly strangling her from within.

Madame Duvalle took a pinch of snuff from the enamel box she kept in her reticule and seemed unaware of Louisa's angry stare. Only when the men came in to join them did she return her gaze to her sewing.

The gentlemen were in good humour, due in great measure, she suspected, to the empty bottle they would have left in the dining-room.

Madame Duvalle immediately patted the seat by her side, saying, 'Come Rossington, sit here and tell me how many geese you have shot today.'

'Are you truly interested, *madame?*' he responded.

'Whatever you have to say is of interest to me, *mon chér.*'

'Lady Rossington must do us the honour

of playing a little Mozart,' Mr. Hopewell declared.

'Oh, indeed, she must,' Sir Max rejoined.

Louisa looked up in a way which was unusually flirtatious for her. 'Do you think I play so well, Sir Max?'

'It would be unchivalrous of me to deny it, my lady, but I must also confess the selfish urge to be near you to have the honour of turning the pages of your music. That to me is the greater pleasure by far.'

She glanced then at her husband who was now in deep conversation with Sophie Duvalle before turning back to Sir Max and laughing gaily.

'I could not be so heartless as to refuse.'

She put down her sewing and allowed him to escort her to the harpsichord. As she sat down on the stool she glanced at her husband once again. Anger kindled within her once more when she realised he didn't even realise Sir Max was flirting with her in the most blatant way. He was behaving rather blatantly himself.

When she looked away again Sir Max was smiling at her in a knowing manner she hated to see, and as she brought her hands down on the keyboard they created only a discordant sound.

Eleven

They were walking in the garden which was bare and bleak, and a cold wind was blowing in from the sea, but that did not deter the couple strolling as if it were midsummer. Warmly wrapped in a fur-lined cloak, Madame Duvalle seemed unaware of the cold.

Standing at the window of her drawing-room, Louisa watched her husband and the woman she knew to be more than his cousin, walking arm-in-arm, deep in conversation, their heads close together.

In her heart a wind icier than the one blowing outside raged through her. Seeing them together like this caused her to shake with emotion. He had never devoted time to her in this way, although she recognised he had never promised to do anything other than give her his name and an establishment of her own. Foolishly she had believed that was all she wanted, for no one ever to pity her again, and yet here she was the most pitiful of all creatures—a woman who loved in vain. How ironic it was that she loved this man. It seemed she must have loved him all the time to accept the marriage on his terms, which were becoming more intolerable with each day that passed.

There came a knock on the door, and when she turned away from the window, Sir Max came into the room.

'I am indeed the most fortunate of men to have found you at last.'

She smiled faintly. No longer could his flattery rally her. In fact she was beginning to find his persistence repulsive.

'I thought you might be with the bra...Lord Danby,' he amended quickly.

'So I was...earlier.'

'I trust I do not intrude.'

Recalling her duties, she injected more warmth into her voice. 'Not at all, Sir Max. How may I be of service to you?'

He came across the room. 'Dear lady, do not tempt me to tell you.' He moved the curtain a fraction and stared down at the very scene which had so distressed her. 'The good weather holds,' he murmured before releasing the curtains.

Louisa moved away from him. 'Do you enjoy your stay at Trevarrick?' she asked in a voice which was unnaturally high.

'Far more than any visit I have made anywhere in my life.'

She laughed uneasily then. 'What flummery, Sir Max. I scarce think the amenities at Trevarrick as so great to warrant such enthusiasm.'

'To me the amenities could not be better. The presence of a beautiful woman is enough to please me, but then,' he added, waving his hand in the air, 'I am but a simple soul. My only criticism is that you are not to be seen as often as I would wish. Your company is so delightful.'

She smiled uncertainly, holding on to the back of a chair. 'Sir Max, you must know I spend a deal of my time with my husband's son.'

'And he is, I am persuaded, quite undeserving and indifferent to your charms.' She moved away, but he followed and took her hand in his. 'You really should not be allowed to suffer those who do not appreciate your qualities, Lady Rossington. You are deserving of a man who would treat you with the honour and affection you deserve.'

His meaning was unmistakable. He raised her hands to his lips. 'You and

I, Lady Rossington, have a rare rapport. I felt it the moment we met.'

She had no chance to pull away before the door opened and a rather breathless Jenny came in. When she saw Sir Max holding Louisa's hands she grew pale and began to stammer her apologies. Sir Max gasped with annoyance at the intrusion, but on Louisa's part she had never been so glad to see anyone.

'What is amiss, girl?' she asked breathlessly, disengaging her hands at last.

'Beggin' yer pardon, my lady, but I had to come...'

'That is quite all right. In matters pertaining to Lord Danby I am always available. Is something wrong with him?'

'He won't eat his food, ma'am.'

'Because he is ill?'

'No, my lady. He just won't eat. There's nought wrong with him that I can see.'

Hesitating only momentarily she addressed Sir Max who was still looking vexed. 'Pray excuse me, Sir Max. I must go to the nursery.'

'He is in need of a good thrashing,' Sir Max answered darkly. 'You are too lenient with him and I shall tell Rossington so.'

'If you wish to be my friend, Sir Max,

you will do nothing of the kind.'

He inclined his head. 'I am your servant, my lady.'

She hurried Jenny from the room, saying in a low voice, 'This is nothing you have not encountered before. Allow him to go hungry and he will eat soon enough.'

It was a most opportune interruption, and she was inclined more to kiss Nicholas rather than scold him.

'But he asks for something in place of his mutton, and I don't know what it is.'

The child was sitting facing a full plate, his arms folded before him in a stubborn stance Louisa recognised all too well.

'Why won't you eat this, Nicholas,' she asked immediately. 'You've always enjoyed your mutton and carrots before.'

'I want something different, that's all. I'm tired of mutton and beef, and I loathe rabbit pie.'

'What in particular would you prefer? Perchance I can arrange for you to have it on another day if you eat what is put before you today.'

'*Blinis*. I want a *blini*—with caviare,' he added in a challenging voice.

'See, my lady. Heathen food it is, you mark my words.'

'Hush now, Jenny. Let his lordship explain to us what this dish is like and perchance Cook will be able to prepare it for him.'

'She'll have the vapours more like,' came the muttered reply.

'A *blini* is a *blini*,' claimed the boy with mounting frustration. 'What else can it be?'

Turning on her heel, Louisa left the room, saying, 'I shall find out, but I want to see that plate empty when I return.

'Has Lord Rossington returned yet?' she asked of the footman when she came downstairs.

'A few minutes ago, my lady. He's at present in the library...'

She hurried there immediately, but drew back in the doorway when she saw that the earl was not alone. Madame Duvalle was still with him, smiling up at him as he bent over her.

For a few seconds the scene, like a portrait, seemed to freeze before her eyes. The sight of them together, Sophie Duvalle's auburn head so close to his dark one, caused her own heart to fill with pain.

When she entered the room he drew

169

away, and Louisa did not miss the look of irritation which crossed his face. Madame Duvalle, however, was smiling.

As well she might, Louisa fumed inwardly. At that moment there was murder in her heart, so much so that her emotions frightened her.

'Louisa?' the earl asked in a voice so detached it wounded her deeply, being quite different to the way he addressed Sophie Duvalle.

'Pardon the intrusion,' she said at last; anger made her breathless and her voice was uneven in consequence.

'I trust that the need is an urgent one.'

'Don't be a goose, Rossington,' Madame Duvalle murmured. 'Lady Rossington does not need an urgent reason to speak with you. I assure you, our business was of no consequence.'

She got up and walked to the window, Louisa's eyes followed every movement, and then she returned her attention to the earl and was dismayed to detect a look of amusement on his face as if he were well aware of her irritation.

'Nicholas is asking for something called a *blini* and none of us knows what it is.'

He stared at her in disbelief for a

moment or two before he said, 'Is he, by jove?'

'I was persuaded you were the only one who might know what it is.'

'But what, may I ask, is wrong with good English beef and mutton?'

'Nothing, he owns, but he wants a *blini*-with caviare,' she added lamely, feeling that she was on a fool's errand.

She stole a glance at Madame Duvalle, who was now watching them both, an amused smile on her lips. No doubt they both thought her a fool, indulging a small child in this way.

'Your son, Rossington, reminds me painfully of his father,' Madame Duvalle said at last. 'When he wants something nothing is allowed to get in his way.'

Louisa wondered if there was some significance in her words, but was immediately diverted by her husband's laughter.

'Mayhap you are correct, my dear. Well, he shall have one.'

'I still don't know what it is,' Louisa told him, feeling now that she was, somehow, being excluded from their joke.

'A *blini* is a kind of pancake, usually filled with meat, but Nicholas has excellent taste; he wants sturgeon's roe in his.'

Louisa smiled uncertainly. 'Meat will have to suffice, but I will tell Cook. I am sorry to have intruded.'

She withdrew and paused outside the library door to draw in a deep breath. It was surprising to discover his son's peccadilloes amused the earl for once, so she supposed Madame Duvalle's presence had to be a good influence on him, in some respects at least.

As Christmastide approached the atmosphere at Trevarrick became even lighter. Louisa was adept to keeping her feelings to herself, vowing that she would never humiliate herself by admitting them to her husband, who, she was sure, would only be amused.

Roving bands of entertainers called in at the house to entertain the inhabitants, servants and master alike. They were, of course, handsomely rewarded for their efforts and given food and ale before going on their way. Wassailers and handbell ringers from the villages nearby came to sing traditional tunes and then partook of plum pudding and mulled ale before moving on. Louisa was particularly pleased for Nicholas, who was seeing it all for the first time. Amy's children took such events very much for granted.

A band of mummers acted out the traditional Christmas play, and Louisa was very gratified when Nicholas clung on to her at a particularly frightening part of the action when the Dragon was about to be slain.

With her arms about him, she glanced at her husband in time to see Madame Duvalle whisper something which made him laugh. She supposed she ought to be satisfied that she had achieved a success with Nicholas in so short a time, for she knew he would be well satisfied with that and it was the most she could hope for.

The mummers' play was well appreciated, and travelling with them were a troupe of acrobats whose act followed the play. They were lively and agile, and Nicholas clapped with excitement at their antics. All too soon the climax of the performance came with one tumbler leaping head over heels down the sweeping curve of the staircase.

Everyone gasped and then fell into silence as he began, but the hush was soon broken quite unexpectedly by Nicholas screaming, 'Mama!' shrilly until he fell into a dead faint in Louisa's arms.

'Shall I summon a physician from Truro?' the earl asked worriedly as he laid his insensible son down on the bed.

'Not yet,' Louisa told him. 'It is only a swoon, I'm persuaded. He will recover soon.' She looked up at him. 'You had best return to your guests. I'll remain with him, and if I deem it necessary to summon a physician I shall send word.'

Looking heart sick he nodded, and Louisa watched him until he had gone. With the aid of her vinaigrette the child soon recovered his senses, but he clung on to Louisa for a long time, and she did not think to leave him until he had been asleep for some time.

'Don't hesitate to summon me back if he needs me at any time,' she cautioned Jenny before she left.

'Poor mite. I wonder what frightened him so?'

'I wonder,' Louisa echoed.

In the hall the servants were putting chairs back in their rightful place and snuffing candles. For once the house party must have retired earlier than usual, for no sounds of jollity issued forth from the side-rooms. The absence of the others was a relief to Louisa who hesitated, wondering what she should do next. Certainly the last thing she wanted was to go to bed. Her mind was far too active to contemplate that, however late the hour.

The earl must have been watching for her, for as she came into the hall he stepped out of the library.

'How is he?' he asked anxiously.

'Sleeping normally now.'

'That is a great relief,' he said averting his eyes.

She went past him and into the library, noting that the decanter on his desk was half empty. The fire had been made up and fresh candles placed in the sconces and candlesticks.

'I owe you an explanation,' he said as a footman closed the door behind them.

'Yes, it is time I was given one. I don't wish to discuss it with Nicholas.'

'The answers you obtain from him might not be to your liking,' he answered grimly.

She sat down in the chair she had last seen occupied by Madame Duvalle, and the memory afflicted her sorely.

He refilled his glass before saying, 'Nicholas is obviously haunted by the memory of his mother's death.'

Louisa looked away. 'I see.'

'No, you do not. Natalia did not die in bed. She...fell to her death.' Louisa looked away, and he went on, 'Nicholas saw her fall.'

'No doubt during a bout of her insanity,' Louisa supplied.

'No!' He looked truly horrified, and Louisa felt bound to say, 'I beg your pardon if I am in error, but I wish to be clear on everything, and I did hear that she was insane.'

'From whom?' She didn't answer, so he did so for her. 'Madame Duvalle.'

'She knows, it seems, more than I.'

He was angry now. 'She does not. She knows nothing, Louisa. I have only spoken of the matter in passing, I assure you. It is true Natalia's mother was insane and because of it her father indulged her too much. In consequence she was spoilt and capricious, often difficult, but quite, quite sane, I assure you.'

Louisa sat forward in her chair. 'Had she lived she might have become insane like her mother.'

'I see no reason to suppose it,' he answered stiffly.

'Rohan, I beg of you to be honest with me at last. Is that not why you wanted me here? To guard your son should he too become insane!'

He looked genuinely aghast. 'No! Louisa, you mustn't believe that.'

'I believe Nicholas is as sane as I am, but he is not just haunted by his mother's fall to her death. Rohan, you have been less than frank with me even now.'

Again he looked away. 'Natalia's foot caught in the hem of her gown. She was unable to save herself. I was there too, but it happened too quickly for me to do anything to prevent her falling. Nicholas came on the scene seconds later to see his mother lying dead at the foot of the stairs and me at the top, looking down on her. It is not difficult to know his thoughts.'

'Nor is he the only one from all accounts.' He gave her a sharp look, and she went on, a little shamefacedly. 'My sister wrote of rumours circulating in St. Petersburg.'

He put down his glass and got to his feet then. 'Did she indeed? How kind of her. No doubt you and she have decided the truth of the matter in your own minds, just as my son has.'

Louisa looked at him in horror at being misinterpreted in this way. 'No, Rohan. No. That isn't...'

His smile became a sneer. 'Oh no? Well, I am not known as a man of honour. You know that as well as I.' Again she looked away. 'What possible motive could I have for killing poor Natalia? The lovers she had? Her impossible temper? No! Of course,' he said, turning to face her, 'it was her money, wasn't it? The commodity I would do anything to possess.'

'No one has made an accusation, I promise you.' she protested.

His face was livid. 'Nothing so brave as a direct accusation. Innuendoes will suffice. Well, my dear Louisa, you may rest in your bed at night, knowing that I have no such motive for doing away with *you.*'

He flung open the door and strode out. Louisa tried to call his name, but managed only to utter a strangled sob. Somewhere she heard a door slam as sobs began to rack her body, and she buried her face in her hands in a vain attempt to blot out the ugliness which seemed to pervade her life.

Twelve

Nicholas recovered his fright far more quickly than Louisa from her subsequent encounter with his father. For most of the time she was unbearably sad. It seemed what brief rapport they had enjoyed was destroyed for ever, for he devoted even more time than before to Madame Duvalle and his two gentlemen guests. Louisa wished they would go, although she was aware there was little chance of regaining an easy relationship with him again. In any event, once the visitors were gone they were like to be even more ill at ease with each other. The presence of guests at least alleviated some of the awkwardness.

The turn of the year came and went, and the visitors made no declaration about leaving. Even Nicholas was moved to question it one day in the schoolroom after he saw his father ride away with the woman Louisa regarded as his paramour.

'When will Madame Duvalle leave, *matouchka?*'

'I really couldn't say,' she answered with a sigh, glancing out of the window, wishing she could have been the woman at his side. Perhaps she will never leave, she said to herself.

There was a light dusting of snow on the ground, but the weather remained remarkably good for the time of the year. Spring, she had been told, came early to the peninsula, and already wild flowers were pushing their way through the heath and gorse which surrounded Trevarrick.

Suddenly Louisa closed the book neither she nor Nicholas could concentrate on, and got to her feet.

'Are you angry with me, *matouchka?*' he asked anxiously, and she gave him a reassuring smile.

'No, but I don't see why we should stay indoors whilst the weather is still so clement. There will be time for your studies when the snow comes. Let's take Rollo for a walk this morning, before he grows fat and lazy.'

The boy was enthusiastic except for one point. 'But will he not run away, *matouchka?*'

'One of the servants will procure a length of twine, or a leather thong if we're lucky.

We may as well go now. There is no knowing when the snow will come.'

'In St. Petersburg we have lots of snow and the Neva freezes over so we can skate on it.'

'That must be very nice. It doesn't happen very often in England, but there are those who remember walking on the Thames during winters past.'

Louisa felt immediately better once she felt the cold air on her face. In truth, she would have preferred to ride if she had not been so afraid of coming across the earl, and also with Nicholas for company it would be impossible to gallop freely as she wished.

At least the child seemed happy with his new pet, and that was a great comfort. Rollo pulled him along, and Louisa, hampered by her full skirts and cloak, struggled to keep up with them.

'Which way shall we go?' she called when they reached the bridle-path. 'Do you think Rollo would like to visit the creek?'

'Let's go to Mr. Harden's and show Rollo off to his brothers and sisters.'

'Mr. Harden's house is a long way from here.'

181

'Not if we take the short cut. I know where it is.'

Rollo tugged Nicholas along, and Louisa began to follow. There was, after all, no hurry to return to Trevarrick.

'Nicholas,' she said after they'd been walking a while, 'you don't have so many nightmares any more.' He didn't answer, and she went on in a gentle voice, 'Are you happier at Trevarrick now?'

'I like it much better since you came.'

That admission gave her a great deal of satisfaction, but she had not asked in order to feed her own vanity.

'You know, Nicholas,' she said in a careful tone a few moments later, 'our eyes sometimes deceive us. We don't always see what we think we see, rather as it was with the jugglers who came at Christmastide. They seemed to perform miraculous tasks, but it wasn't quite so. Your Mama fell, Nicholas. It was an accident. No one pushed her.'

The boy's face took on an agonised look. '*Matouchka*, I *saw* him.'

'He saw you too, which only meant that he was there just as you were. That's all. Don't you think it possible that you were mistaken after all?'

182

'Yes, but...'

'Think about it, Nicholas. It's very wrong to accuse someone unjustly. I know it pains your Papa very much you think him guilty of such a terrible crime.'

He didn't say anything, and Louisa knew there was nothing more she could do. The last thing she wanted was to cause him more distress, but this conversation had to be broached. Now it was ended—she would not speak of it again although she wasn't certain she had helped.

The path sloped gently downwards away from Trevarrick through a copse where birds scattered before them as they walked. Every now and again flurries of snow blew in their faces, and after they had been walking a while Louisa felt bound to say to the unusually silent boy.

'I think we should go back, Nicholas, before the weather turns nasty. Rollo can see his relatives another day.'

The boy frowned. 'This is nothing. In Russia it *really* snows, but I am not so certain Mr. Harden's house is this way after all. I've never been here before. Perhaps we should have taken that other path.'

'Never mind. I own it has been an

enjoyable walk, and I'm persuaded Rollo has enjoyed it too. We shall come out again and make certain we go to Mr. Harden's next time.'

'There's a cottage over there, *matouchka*. I wonder who it belongs to.'

Louisa turned again, and it was true there was a cottage at the far side of the copse. 'I don't know either. It's certainly too small to be a dowerhouse.'

'Perhaps someone there will give us tea and muffins,' he suggested, which made her laugh.

'I would not depend upon it, my dear.'

'We cannot leave without seeing.'

'Well, I suppose you are entitled to discover who lives on Trevarrick land.'

She took his hand in hers and they walked briskly towards the cottage which had a small garden in front and a briar rose entwined round the porch. As they approached she noticed that a wisp of smoke was coming from the chimney, but there was no response to their knock.

They were just about to walk away from the cottage, back towards Trevarrick, when the sound of pounding hooves caused Louisa to hold Nicholas back. Moments later a solitary horseman came riding through the copse, someone she recognised immediately.

'Why, it is Mr. Logan, Nicholas.'

He reined in the moment he saw them, dismounting and tethering his horse to the fence. Bowing low he said, 'Lady Rossington, Lord Danby, what a happy chance.'

'How nice to see you again, Mr. Logan.'

'The pleasure is all mine, my lady,' and from the look on his face and his tone Louisa knew that to be true. 'You are somewhat far from Trevarrick.'

'Rollo has been taking us for a walk,' she explained, laughing as she did so. 'We were just about to turn back when we caught sight of this cottage and we were wondering who lived here when you came along so fortuitously.'

'The cottage is mine, Lady Rossington.'

She laughed again and said to Nicholas, 'That at least solves the mystery. Do you live here alone, Mr. Logan?'

'With my mother when she is at home, but at present she is visiting my sister in Penzance.'

'So you are not married,' she felt bound to ask.

He smiled wryly. 'Alas no.'

185

'If you regret it, surely the remedy is obvious.'

'My desires in that direction are invariably thwarted, Lady Rossington, for the best ladies by far are already wed.'

The way he was looking at her made her blush, and Nicholas asked then in his innocence, 'Do you have any muffins, Mr. Logan?'

Both he and Louisa laughed, and she scolded, 'You mustn't ask, Nicholas.'

'If only I had such a delicacy they would all be yours, dripping with butter too. But I do have some marchpane, if you would care to step inside.'

'Oh, yes please.'

He led the way down the path, and after he had opened the door stood back to allow them to enter. The parlour seemed very tiny to Louisa who was accustomed to the large rooms of Trevarrick. The ceiling beams were low, causing her to duck her head although she had no need to.

Immediately he ushered her to a chair near the fire and then proceeded to throw some logs onto the dying embers.

'You must be chilled to the bone, Lady Rossington.'

'We have been walking briskly, but this

186

respite is most welcome, I own.'

'If ever you are passing and I am not at home, please feel free to come in and warm yourself. The door is never on the latch, and if my mother is here you may be sure she will be delighted to welcome you.'

She flushed with pleasure. 'That is very kind of you, Mr. Logan.'

He straightened up. 'Now where is that marchpane?'

'Oh, please do not trouble, Mr. Logan.'

'He promised,' Nicholas pointed out, whilst Rollo sniffed suspiciously around the room.

After a few moments Mark Logan brought out a box of marchpane from the dresser and gave it to the delighted boy.

'You may go round to the back and feed the hens if you wish,' he told him, and, calling to Rollo to hurry, the child ran out of the cottage.

'He really is quite a different child to the one who came here,' he told her when Nicholas had gone.

'Was he truly so bad?'

He laughed. 'Quite shocking, I fear, Lady Rossington. He plagued everyone in the house and quite a few who were outside it. Only loyalty to Lord Rossington ensured that they remained and endured it.'

Louisa smiled faintly. 'It was a foolish question. He misbehaved most dreadfully on that first night, and on subsequent occasions.'

'He couldn't fail to respond to you, though. No one should be surprised at the improvement in his manners.'

'I am a little too indulgent with him, and I fear that Rossington will soon call a halt.'

'Kindness will never come amiss, and Lord Rossington would be the first person to acknowledge that,' he answered before adding. 'And it was kind of you to arrange such splendid gifts of food for all the tenants, Lady Rossington.'

She blushed again. She had not sought male admiration for many years, and now it had come so late and from the wrong people she was at a loss how to cope.

'When I engaged a nursemaid for Lord Danby I realised how hard life could be for most of these people.'

'The incumbents in these parts manage rather better than most. There is always a cask of brandy or a chest of tea to exchange for food and clothing when the need arises.'

She laughed, something which came easily to her in this man's company. 'So I understand. Mrs. Pendas told me a cask of brandy, or tea, is always left at Trevarrick after a landing. I confess I was, at first, horrified, especially as my husband is a magistrate, but it appears no one thinks it amiss.'

'Indeed not, ma'am. Perchance you will allow me to offer you a glass of ratafia from my own plentiful stock.'

She laughed again, amazed how at ease she was with this man in a way she could not be with Sir Max, and certainly not with the earl. Her pleasure only served to remind her of the tension she now felt at Trevarrick, dreading to set eyes upon him and yet longing to do so.

Afraid he would read her thoughts, she averted her eyes, 'No, I thank you, Mr. Logan, and,' she added, getting to her feet, 'I must make haste to return to Trevarrick before it grows dark. I'm so pleased to have seen you.'

She gave him her hand, which he raised to his lips. 'Be certain, my lady, your presence here has transformed a mundane day into one that is very special.'

When he escorted her outside, Louisa

was surprised to find Nicholas sitting quietly on a rustic seat, staring into space, the puppy curled up at his feet.

'That is a very uncommon sight,' Mark Logan observed.

Louisa gazed at him sombrely for a moment or two before explaining, 'We spoke of certain matters on our way here, and I believe he is now thinking on it, which was my intention.'

Just as she turned to bid him a final good bye they both heard a horseman approaching. Rollo began to bark, and Louisa and Mark Logan looked expectantly to see the earl galloping at full speed towards them.

As he was the very last person she expected to see, and alone too, she just stared. The horse scarcely came to a halt before the earl jumped down. Steam billowed from the horse's nostrils which indicated he had been given a hard ride in direct contrast to the sedate canter the earl would have enjoyed with Madame Duvalle.

Mark Logan bowed low, and somehow Louisa felt such subservience became him ill. The earl regarded them both darkly, and she was surprised again, this time to note he was angry about something.

'Louisa,' he said, greeting her with extreme curtness. In addition there was a coldness in his eye.

'This is a pleasant surprise,' she answered, feeling foolish, for it did give her a great deal of pleasure to see him so unexpectedly, so much so her heart began beating wildly. Then she added shyly, 'I did not look to see you here.'

'No doubt,' he answered with no warmth whatsoever, 'but if you will permit, Logan and I have business to discuss.'

In the face of such persistent coolness, her own warmth faded and she became withdrawn again. 'Of course. How foolish of me to detain you. Good day to you, Mr. Logan.'

'Good day, Lady Rossington,' he responded, and she noted that he frowned, no doubt puzzled by the coolness between a couple so recently wed.

She took hold of the boy's hand and began to walk away. The earl turned on his heel to watch her, his face dark and inscrutible.

Nicholas had been unusually quiet since his father arrived on the scene; perhaps he too had sensed the anger and was puzzled by it.

As they walked through the copse Louisa heard the cottage door slam shut. All pleasure from the encounter had gone.

'*Matouchka,*' Nicholas said after a while, 'why are there tears on your face?'

Louisa quickly dashed them away with her hand before forcing a smile to her lips.

'They are not tears, Nicholas,' she told him, 'just my eyes watering from the cold.'

Thirteen

When they arrived back at Trevarrick, Louisa went straight to her room, and, pleading a headache, excused herself from dinner that night. To face their guests who were always in the highest of spirits, and Madame Duvalle who had every right to be pleased with herself, was beyond her just then. Much less could she bear to witness the earl's attentions to that woman any longer.

192

'You've took a chill, that's what you've done,' Dora complained. 'Walkin' in this cold. Madness, that's what it is.'

'I have not taken a chill,' Louisa assured her, 'nor do I wish for you to cluck around me like a mother hen. I am merely a trifle fatigued and don't wish to take dinner downstairs.'

The maid did not seem convinced, and Louisa dismissed her as soon as was possible. She tried to sleep, but drowsiness refused to overtake her active mind, so eventually she rose from the bed and settled down to read by the fire.

However, the novel could not hold her interest on this occasion. She could not help but think of the party downstairs, complete without her as in the past. She wondered too if the earl actually loved Madame Duvalle, if he were capable of loving any woman. It was not, she realised, her fate to discover that, but the strain of living with him like a stranger was beginning to be unbearable.

The sound of the door to the next room closing with a bang caused her to start, and to realise how late it really was. Almost immediately afterwards the communicating-door to her room opened

193

and she started again to see her husband framed in the doorway.

'I want to talk to you,' he said, and although he did not seem foxed she knew he would have been drinking a good deal during the evening.

'Do you not think it a little late?' she ventured.

'Oh, be damned with the time!' He came into the room, and she drew back in the chair. 'There is little enough time during the day when you are available to me.'

'Nonsense,' she was stung to retort. 'It is you who are fully occupied with your cronies.'

'Well, at least we have discovered how *you* spend your days—at Logan's cottage.'

Shocked she answered, 'Stuff and nonsense! Today was the very first time I had been there, and we came upon it quite by accident.'

His look was a disbelieving one. 'Such innocence. I will not be churlish enough to gainsay it. However, Louisa, you will not go there again unless accompanied by me. Is that understood?'

Her cheeks flamed with anger. 'No, it is not. Why should I not pass the time of day

194

with Mr. Logan when I am in the vicinity of his cottage?'

'Because I do not wish you to.'

'That would be exceeding uncivil of me.'

He began to pace up and down the room, clasping and unclasping his hands behind his back. 'Louisa, you cannot be so obtuse you do not know why I make this stipulation.'

She was growing even more angry then, jumping to her feet and clasping her shawl about her. 'You make yourself very clear, but do you truly suppose I should have taken Nicholas with me on an assignation, for that is what you accuse me of.'

A look of irritation crossed his face. 'I accuse you of nothing. I can readily see, however, the danger of such a practice, moreover what the tattle-baskets would make of it too. We have a position to maintain, and you must behave with dignity at all times.'

Louisa wrung her hands together. 'What humbug! Is it more acceptable for Sir Max to attempt to make love to me beneath this very roof and in front of you?'

He stared at her in astonishment, and it was clear he had no notion. After a moment he snapped, 'Has he behaved improperly towards you?'

She lowered her eyes. 'No, but that is because I have given him no opportunity. His intentions are very clear, but he is a gentleman is he not? His behaviour is deemed natural, whereas Mr. Logan...'

Her anger began to mount again as he turned on his heel and strode back across the room. His disregard of her, and her feelings, almost caused her to choke.

'Enough has been said on this matter. I will not broach the subject again, but you will heed me in this matter, Louisa.'

'Oh, you *are* a humbug, Rohan! How dare you castigate me on such an innocent occurrence when you invite your paramour into our home—my home too, for good or ill—and use some flimsy excuse of kinship to install her in one of your London houses.'

Her words were enough to halt him halfway across the room, and as he turned on his heel Louisa was half afraid she had gone too far, but she felt goaded beyond bearing.

'What did you say?' he asked, coming back towards her.

Louisa clutched her shawl even closer

around her. 'I believe you heard me perfectly well.'

'She is my cousin,' he said in a low, well-controlled voice.

'Tush! She is your lightskirt, and neither of you have made much pretence to hide it. I am not so green I'd believe that Banbury Tale, if indeed you intended me to do so.'

He let out a long breath. 'If that is so, why should so commonplace a matter trouble you, Louisa? The presence of my lightskirt would in no way incommode you, my dear.'

She averted her eyes, all bravado gone now. 'You deliberately humiliate me.'

'By jove,' he said with a wry smile. 'Do I detect a glimmer of jealousy escaping from that cold heart of yours? If you object, you have only to say so, I assure you. It would not be distasteful to me to alter the terms of our marriage. Mayhap, now Nicholas is better behaved you find life here monotonous.'

He took a step forward, and she flinched away. His eyes gleamed with what appeared to be malice. 'No? Mayhap, I have a mind to alter the state which is becoming more unsatisfactory, whether you wish it or not.

Especially when I am obliged to witness the way you flaunt your charms before other men.'

Louisa pushed her hair back from her face with trembling hands. 'That is an untruth.' He took another few steps towards her, and moving back, she cried, 'You would not be so dishonourable as to go back on our arrangement.'

He stopped advancing on her, but her relief was short-lived. 'Would I not? You surely wouldn't be surprised if I did, Louisa? A man who would abandon his betrothed and even perhaps do away with his wife would have no scruples. Why should I not have what is by rights mine? Tell me that, Louisa?'

She pressed her hand to her lips, unaware that she was sinking her teeth into the flesh. Then, gasping back a sob, she turned away from him again. 'I have done all you asked of me. Nicholas is happier than when I arrived, his manners improved...'

'You have done well with him, that I shall not deny, and I have fulfilled my part of the agreement. You have everything you wish, everything that I promised would be yours, so do not seek to tell me with whom I should or should not consort.'

She looked at him sharply, hating to see the cruel look on his face. 'I did not.'

'You seem to take amiss the presence of Madame Duvalle in this house, but you should not for when I made the offer of marriage I did not vow a lifelong fidelity. You surely did not expect me to take an oath of celibacy with our marriage vows. As you will readily agree, the marriage was purely for appearances' sake, so you could care for Nicholas.'

As he spoke so dispassionately with all his anger gone, Louisa found she was, herself, shaking with rage.

'You scarce need to remind me of the circumstances of our marriage, but I fail to see why our agreement should be one-sided, or indeed why you should care if I take a lover.'

He caught hold of her by the arm and swung her round to face him. Although trembling with emotion herself, she knew she had never seen him so angry before. His eyes seemed to be aflame with anger, and his skin pale by comparison.

'I will not be cuckolded by my own land-steward.'

Louisa's eyes blazed into his. 'Am I to

assume your painted crony would be more acceptable?'

His face twisted into a grimace of rage. 'You doxy.'

Before she had a chance to realise what he was about to do he had slapped her hard across her cheek. Her head snapped back, and as he released his grip on her she stumbled and fell against the chair. Louisa was unable to save herself, nor did she make any attempt to do so. She sank to the floor, sobbing bitterly, hiding her enflamed cheek with her hand.

Immediately he was on his knees beside her, saying anxiously, 'Louisa? Are you hurt?'

'Go away,' she sobbed. 'I beg you, go away.'

'I'm so sorry. I didn't intend to hurt you. Please forgive me.'

He tried to help her to her feet, but still sobbing heartbrokenly she resisted all his efforts.

'Louisa, please say you will forgive me?' he begged, and she raised her eyes to look at him at last. 'You may do as you wish, for I have no right to make any demands on you.'

He brushed the hair away from her face

and pulled her close to him. She knew he was going to kiss her, and she was powerless to resist when he pressed his lips to her cheek where he had hit her.

Louisa was too surprised to do anything save allow it to happen. His lips brushed hers then before becoming more insistent. Despite her instinctive urge to draw away, a response stirred inside her, a feeling repressed for so long. The feeling grew stronger, and she was able to forget that minutes earlier they had faced each other with hatred in their hearts. For too long she had held back, and now she experienced a rush of emotion such as she had never known before. Her own arms went around him, and no longer was she passive as his kisses began to bruise her with their strength.

'Matouchka.'

The earl drew away from her abruptly, cursing beneath his breath, and Louisa got to her feet at last when she saw Nicholas standing in the doorway in his nightshirt. His face was pale and his eyes were wide with fear.

Without looking back Louisa hurried towards him, her mind still half-dazed at those kisses and their effect upon her.

She hurried him out of the room and down the corridor, scolding, 'Nicholas, what are you doing out of bed at this time of night?'

'I had one of those bad dreams again.'

'It's over now, so you can go back to sleep.'

She put her arm around his shoulders and led him back to his room, where, no doubt, Jenny would be sleeping soundly. When they reached it she drew a sigh and could not stifle the wish that on this night of all nights Nicholas had not had one of his bad dreams.

Fourteen

By the time he fell asleep again and Louisa was able to return to her room she was not surprised to discover the earl gone. It had taken some time to reassure the child that his father had not been trying to hurt her. She could only be glad he had not arrived five minutes earlier when their argument had been in full flow. It scarcely bore thinking about the effect of witnessing him striking her would have had on the boy.

The communicating-door was firmly shut and, throwing her shawl down, she climbed wearily into bed at last. But she could not sleep. Her mind was not dwelling upon the slap which had made her head reel, but her body ached to be held against his once again, to give rein to the passion she knew now had been held back for too long.

When she awoke the following morning, her instincts told her immediately it was much later than was usual. She got quickly out of bed on hearing noises, horses, outside.

Pulling back the curtain she was in time to see a procession of carriages making their way along the drive from the house. A thin layer of snow had fallen during the night, but not enough to muffle the movements of the horses.

She allowed the curtain to fall back into place and then hurried to the fireplace where she tugged at the bell-pull. After that she went to the dressing-table and carefully inspected her face in the mirror for the first time.

There was, she discovered, no mark upon her cheek where he had struck her, but there was a bruise where her face had hit the chair. Fortunately it could easily be disguised by rouge and a patch.

Louisa was searching her patch-box for a suitable one when Dora came in with hot water.

'What is going on in this house today?' Louisa demanded.

'Beggin' your pardon, ma'am, but his lordship gave orders for you not to be disturbed.'

Louisa was surprised, but gave no sign of it before asking, 'Which of our guests have departed this morning, Dora?'

'All of them, ma'am,' the girl replied as she poured the water into the wash-bowl. 'Mayhap before the snow grows too deep.'

It was as Louisa had wished for so long, but she could no longer rejoice in their departure for whatever reason, for overriding any gladness she might feel was a dread of her next encounter with the earl. How she could face him after last night she did not know. How she could hide her longing for him was going to be a greater test, for pride would prevent her showing her feelings after his show of contempt, and that was all it had been. Her cheeks flamed with the knowledge he had attempted to use her as a common doxy with no regard for tenderness. That she had responded with such eagerness ensured her future outward coolness towards him, but she so wished it could be otherwise.

The household, when she went downstairs at last, was still in something of an upheaval, and Louisa was glad of that too. Giving instructions to various servants rendered less time for her own troubled thoughts. Her carefree times living with the Mulcasters seemed a distant haven now, and yet she knew she would never wish to return to it. Living with the earl, even though it be in the strained circumstances, was better than not being near to him at all.

As the day progressed she caught not so much as a glimpse of her husband, and finally was forced to enquire of Jenkins about the earl's movements.

'His lordship has been ensconced in the library all day, ma'am.'

'Alone?'

'Mr. Logan was here for a while, but I do believe he has departed.'

After the house-steward had returned to

his duties, Louisa remained in the hall for a while. Eventually she strode across to the library and knocked on the door.

From within came the faint order to enter, and after hesitating a moment longer went in.

He was sitting at the desk, and one glance at least reassured her that she was not disturbing him in anything important. His booted feet were resting on the desk-top and a half-empty glass stood at his elbow.

When she entered his feet slid to the ground and he straightened up, seemingly surprised to see her. Uncertain again now she walked slowly into the room.

'I trust I do not disturb you in anything important.'

'Only in my drinking if that can be deemed important.'

'Our guests have departed very suddenly, have they not?'

He smiled faintly. 'The sight of snow made them realise the possibility of being marooned here.'

He got to his feet and came towards her. 'How is Nicholas today? Convinced I am attempting to make away with you now?'

Her eyes opened wide. 'Indeed he is not.'

His face softened then, and unexpectedly he reached out to brush her cheeks with his fingers.

'You are hiding a bruise beneath that patch.'

Turning her cheek, his hand dropped to his side again.

'It is of no account.'

'Such a lack of control was a rare lapse on my part. You may rest assured it will not happen again.'

She looked at him then, all embarrassment gone in the face of his humility. 'It was as much my fault. That is what I have come to say. I goaded you and quite unnecessarily too. I have no intention of taking a lover, much less Mr. Logan.'

He walked back to the desk and refilled his glass to the rim. 'My dear, he wouldn't dare become your lover however tempting that might be. He knows me too well and values his position here too much.'

She smiled bitterly. 'Such flattery of my charms, Rohan. Take heed lest I be overcome.'

She strode across the room, angry once more. It was far worse than she had envisaged; they could not even converse with a degree of civility any longer.

'If only, Louisa,' he said in a thoughtful tone, 'you could have been satisfied with my love all those years ago.' She turned to look at him curiously as he went on, 'Don't look like that. The world believes I betrayed you, but you and I know you ended our betrothal. It was not I, but have you ever wondered what life for us might be like now if you hadn't written me that note ending our betrothal?' She didn't answer, and he continued, 'I would not, of course, have met Natalia, and there would be no Nicholas, which I would regret. However,' he added, turning his back to her, 'we might well have had children of our own.'

Louisa wanted to say something, but no words would come. More than anything she wanted to prevent him saying more.

'It might amuse you to know I never stopped loving you, however many women sought my attention. Whatever I did to put you out of my mind was unsuccessful. Even Natalia suspected she did not possess my wholehearted love.'

He went back to the desk and, opening one of the drawers, brought out a sheet of paper which he threw towards her.

'I still have it. There. I'll wager you do not even remember what you wrote, whereas I know every word. I read it whenever I begin to think there is an ounce of warmth in you for me.'

Unwillingly and with trembling fingers Louisa picked up the parchment. The writing was painfully familiar and the date almost ten years earlier.

'My dear Lord Rossington,' she read, 'I beg you forgive me writing to you in this manner, but I believe it best not to delay further. I cannot in all conscience become your wife and discharge my duties as such in a way you deserve. There is another whom I love and therefore, Lord Rossington, I pray you will forgive me and know it to be the best course for a happy future for both of us. Your servant, Louisa Farnham.'

Tears were streaming down her face as she let the parchment fall back onto the desk.

'I have distressed you again,' he said gently. 'You must have loved him a great deal. Did he hurt you terribly, Louisa?'

She shook her head, and he went on, 'I have often wondered what manner of man he was to have earned your love as I never could.'

'Stop. Oh, please stop!' she begged.

'It isn't normally in my nature to be self-indulgent about my emotions. You must forgive me, my dear. It will not happen again.'

'Forgive you?' she said through her tears. 'Oh, you don't understand even now. I lied!' The confession was dragged out of her. 'I lied! The entire letter was a falsehood!'

He was staring at her now, not quite knowing what to believe. Shuddering sobs racked her body. She buried her head in her hands, and neither were aware of the commotion in the hall even when there was scuffling outside the library door.

Suddenly the door flew open, and Jenny, accompanied by two footmen who had been attempting to detain her, came stumbling in, distraught, her cloak spotted with snow.

'My lord, my lady,' she cried almost incoherently.

'Lord Danby...Oh, I can't find him!'

Louisa was immediately in control of herself. She turned in horror to the earl who came across the room to grip the girl by the shoulders. He shook her hard as she gulped back a sob.

'What do you mean? Where is he?'

'I don't know, my lord.'

'Where did you last see him then? Come on, girl. Take a hold on your emotions and speak up.'

She looked beseechingly at Louisa. 'He wanted to go out in the snow with the dog, ma'am, and we walked ever such a long way. He was enjoying it so much when he insisted we come back along the headland I hadn't the heart to gainsay him.' She began to sob. 'The dog caught sight of a gull or something and began to give chase. Lord Danby went after him even though I called him back. I ran on too, but I couldn't see him anywhere! He didn't answer my calls either! I called him on and on!'

The colour drained from the earl's face as the girl spoke, and when she finished he let her go. 'The headland. You say you were on the headland?'

'Oh, Rohan, do you think he has fallen off the cliff?' Louisa asked in an agonised voice, oblivious now to her own pain.

'Or down one of the old mine-workings, more like.'

Louisa clapped one hand to her lips, but

the maidservant began to cry out too, and she immediately went to comfort her.

'I looked after him, my lady, honest I did.'

'We know you did, Jenny. No one is blaming you for a child's impetuosity.'

'It's growing dark,' said the earl with obvious agitation. 'and starting to snow again. We must go out and search for him with no further delay.'

He rushed into the hall, calling to the servants and issuing orders the moment they came running.

'I must go too,' wailed Jenny. 'It's all my fault. His lordship'll have my hide for this.'

'Nonsense. Nicholas is headstrong and thoughtless as are most children.'

'I must do *something*, ma'am, or I'll take leave of my senses.'

'You will remain here and put a brick in his bed, but before you do, change out of your own wet clothes. We don't want you to take a chill.' The girl hesitated, and Louisa went on, 'Go upstairs, Jenny, and fetch me a cloak and a pair of stout boots. Go on, do it now. And bring a blanket too.'

By the time the girl returned a small

army of grooms, houseboys, footmen and stable-boys were assembled in the hall, all wearing frieze coats and woolly caps and carrying lighted lanterns.

When the earl came down and found her waiting too, wearing her outdoor clothes, he said, 'What do you think you are doing?'

'I'm coming too, of course.'

'You are to remain here and wait, Louisa.'

'I couldn't,' she answered in an impassioned voice. 'Please let me go with you.'

His face relaxed a little. 'Very well, but the moment you feel at all chilled you are to come back.'

'I can feel only fear until he is safe again,' she admitted.

The moment they left the house the searchers spread out, calling the child's name. There was such a lot of land in which to find one small boy, and there was fear constantly in Louisa's heart.

Night was fast encroaching, and th lanterns illuminated every searcher as they were the piskies who put so mu fear into the hearts of the local inhabita Already they would be blaming the ch disappearance on the piskies, Louisa

213

certain, and, knowing children abducted by the little people were never seen again, she shuddered.

No sound answered their calls. It was snowing again now, and no doubt a further layer had obscured any footprints, making the search that bit more difficult. Somewhere out in the icy darkness he was lying in fear and perhaps pain too. The thought smote at Louisa's heart as she too called out his name in desperation.

'Don't fret, my lady,' Jenkins told her as they stumbled through the snow. 'We'll find him soon enough.'

She could not be comforted though, and it seemed an age before a cry went up. Her heart began to beat unevenly. She glanced at Jenkins, who had been lighting er way with his lantern, and they, like the others, began to hurry as best they d in the direction of the shout.

the time Louisa arrived at what was cured opening to an old tin-mine, a already been lowered by several struggled to keep some purchase ground.

gone down?' she asked spying the earl's valet carry- greatcoat over his arm.

'His lordship, ma'am. Insisted he did even though the most of us volunteered to go in his stead.'

Her heart was once again filled with dread. She might lose them both, now when happiness could be theirs for the taking. A descent such as this was dangerous enough, but on such a night...

'Is it certain Lord Danby is down there?'

'Yes, ma'am,' came the answer. 'Heard him shout myself.'

Louisa clasped her gloved hands together. 'Heaven be praised.'

'He didn't fall all the way, ma'am,' one of the footmen told her. 'His lordship says he's fast on a ledge.'

'That is a relief also,' she gasped, and then she tensed once more as the earl tugged on the rope and the men began to pull with all their might.

Several agonising minutes went by before the earl's head reappeared above the ground, and she could not prevent a cry escaping her lips when she saw Nicholas clinging to him. The child had his arm fast around his father's neck and peepin out of the earl's coat was the irrepressib puppy. She rushed forward, hardly dari to believe they were both safe.

'Oh, Nicholas, you naughty boy,' she said, laughing and crying at the same time as she tucked the blanket around him.

'Rollo fell down the hole,' he explained as if it were a perfectly ordinary occurrence, 'and then I fell down too.'

'Well, you are going home now,' his father told him. 'We've waited too long for our dinner on your account.'

'I'm hungry too,' the child admitted as the earl started back with him towards the house, 'but I suppose I shall be sent to bed without my supper tonight.'

'I think not,' his father replied before Louisa could do so, 'providing, naturally, you give me your word you won't fall down any more mines in the future.'

Realising that he was not to be scolded for the escapade, Nicholas grinned. 'That no hardship. I didn't like it down there neither did Rollo.'

Louisa fell into step at their side and arty walked back to Trevarrick, she 't remember a time she ever felt

ll be served when you are ready, he maidservant told Louisa, who immediately glanced at herself in the cheval mirror.

'Tell Lord Rossington I am ready now,' and then adding to Dora, 'I don't look too hag-ridden, do I?'

'No, my lady. I was only thinking you look radiant tonight. Happen that's because you're relieved to have Lord Danby back safe and sound.'

Louisa frowned at the memory. 'For a while I truly feared we had lost him.'

'Real brave it was of his lordship to go down after him. Could've caved in any time, Jenkins said.'

Louisa cast her a smile. 'Whatever the risk, Dora, he would have taken it.'

'His lordship's sent a case of champagne to the servants' hall too.'

'It is well deserved.'

'As long as his lordship understand we'll all be good and foxed this night.'

Louisa laughed. 'I am persuaded, for once, he will not mind.'

But despite her happiness about Nichol she was apprehensive again when she we downstairs. Throughout the concern Nicholas's safety and the subsequent of finding him unharmed, Louisa had given much thought to the convers which had been interrupted. Now it all came back to her and her heart fluttered with hope and excitement.

'How is he?' the earl asked immediately they took their seats at the dinner-table.

Louisa cast him a quick smile before averting her eyes. 'He is remarkably well, I'm glad to say. He has eaten a hearty meal and I'm persuaded he will suffer no ill effects.'

'That is a great relief.'

Again she smiled faintly across the table. So far she had made no attempt to eat and neither had he despite the tempting array of food presented to them.

'He will recover far more quickly than we, Rohan.' She put down her spoon and fork. 'Nicholas tells me that in Russia rvants do everything for their master you would not have gone after him. A nt would have gone in your stead.'

, very true,' the earl answered v. 'The Russian hierarchy do noth-emselves, even their passage down is usually aided by a footman on

ghed. 'How odd that seems ver, your son declares he is d here and it was you who

218

brought him out of the mine.'

'That,' he answered slowly, 'is very gratifying.' Then, looking down the table at her, he asked, 'Do you not wish to eat?'

'The fright has taken its toll on my appetite, I fear.'

'Mine too.'

He looked at her before asking, 'What did you mean when you said you lied in that letter, Louisa?'

She looked down at her plate. 'There was no other man in my life. You were the one I chose to accept. I will not say it was because of love, for I was at that time unaware of what the emotion really meant, but there was no one but you. There has been no one else and I am bound to say there never will.'

Slowly he got up from his chair, waving to the footman to withdraw from the room.

'Then why...?'

She looked up at him then; her eyes ful of passion. 'It was to allow you to withdra honourably. Papa tricked us both. He l his money and there was no portion my marriage. Oh, I knew you would the honourable thing and marry me in event, but I could not let you make such a noble sacrifice.'

He came down the room, drawing her to her feet when he reached her. 'That was your sole reason?' he asked in wonder.

'None other, I vow. If...if I had suspected you loved me then, nothing would have induced me to write that letter.'

He smiled, and her heart fluttered. 'I must have been remiss in communicating my feelings to you, but be certain I shall remedy that omission from now on.'

Breathlessly she waited for his kiss, and when it came it was the realisation of all her dreams. The restlessness in her heart was stilled for ever.

'I love you,' she whispered against his lips.

When he released her again nevertheless kept his arms close about her, and she murured, 'You might have tried to tell his time.'

ad not the courage. When we met knew I still loved you, but you cold towards me. It seemed I ve no more success on that han nine years earlier, but I ned to bring you back here.' holas as the excuse.'

'I did need help with Nicholas.'

'Which a good governess would have provided.'

'Not so well as you, my love. Have you no notion how your father lost his fortune?'

She sighed. 'He was extravagant in all things, but I believe gaming too deep was the true cause.'

'We are all guilty of that on occasions,' he answered wryly. 'The truth is, Louisa, he did play too deep and lost all his money—to me.'

She looked up at him, her eyes wide. 'Oh no. I had no notion.'

'That was why your father was so anxious for you to marry me. I was the only one who understood—and loved you, naturally. It was a perfect answer to the situation, but after Mr. Farnham died I supposed you ended our betrothal because you were at last free to wed a man more to your taste.'

Louisa was unbearably distressed at hi revelation. 'It was all for nought o unhappiness.'

'We cannot say that, for we are togetl now and we can treasure the happines come all the more for it.'

Her answering smile was a radiant one, and she sighed with contentment as he added, 'Let us hope that the snow will be good and deep for a long time to come so we shall be cut off from the world, and that Nicholas will sleep long too. He has dominated you for far too long.'

She laid her head on his shoulder as his lips brushed her cheek again. 'You may be sure you will have your fair share of my attention from now onwards.'

His grip tightened on her again. 'Oh, indeed I will, Louisa,' he said, and as he kissed her once more she knew the best years of her life were about to begin.

The publishers hope that this book has given you enjoyable reading. Large Print Books are especially designed to be as easy to see and hold as possible. If you wish a complete list of our books, please ask at your local library or write directly to: Dales Large Print Books, Long Preston, North Yorkshire, BD23 4ND, England.

This Large Print Book for the Partially sighted, who cannot read normal print, is published under the auspices of

THE ULVERSCROFT FOUNDATION

THE ULVERSCROFT FOUNDATION

. . . we hope that you have enjoyed this Large Print Book. Please think for a moment about those people who have worse eyesight problems than you . . . and are unable to even read or enjoy Large Print, without great difficulty.

You can help them by sending a donation, large or small to:

**The Ulverscroft Foundation,
1, The Green, Bradgate Road,
Anstey, Leicestershire, LE7 7FU,
England.**
or request a copy of our brochure for more details.

ʼe Foundation will use all your help to ʼst those people who are handicapped ʼ various sight problems and need special attention.

k you very much for your help.